SHAME
ON
HIM

FOOL ME ONCE #3

Also by Tara Sivec

Tara Sivec

SHAME

ON

HIM

FOOL ME ONCE #3

 Montlake
Romance

Published by Montlake Romance, Seattle

www.apub.com

Amazon, the Amazon logo, and Montlake Romance are trademarks of Amazon.com, Inc., or its affiliates.

ISBN-13: 9781477823217
ISBN-10: 1477823212

Cover design by Erin Fitzsimmons

Library of Congress Control Number: 2014900607

Printed in the United States of America

To every woman who has ever been a fool for love. With some handcuffs and booze, you too will find your Prince Charming . . . and kick a little ass along the way.

CHAPTER 1

Your Honor, my client would like to—"
Bzzzzzzzzz.

The vibration of my cell phone forces the device to bounce across the wooden table in front of me. I pause for a moment to glance at the screen and see that it's Paige calling. She knows I'm in court. She also knows I'm not to be interrupted unless someone is dying. With everything that has happened lately—drug lords trying to kill Kennedy, the mob going after Paige—my heart skips a beat.

While opposing counsel is busy stating his case to the court and the judge is looking away, I quickly grab my phone, hunch down in my seat, and bring it to my ear.

"Paige, what's wrong? Is Kennedy okay?" I whisper as softly as I can.

I hear giggling on the other end of the line and then a squeal.

"Paige!" I whisper again, glancing up at Judge Robertson to make sure he's still occupied with the defense.

Another burst of laughter comes through the phone and then Paige finally speaks. "Matt, seriously, that tickles!"

Oh, my God.

"Paige, I'm hanging up now. I'm in court."

"Lorelei! Oh, my gosh, I'm sorry! I totally forgot. I was just calling to remind you that you need to pick up the subpoena today and deliver it to Richard Covington."

"Counselor, are we interrupting something?"

My head whips up and I jerk the phone away from my ear when Judge Robertson bellows across the courtroom at me.

"I'm sorry, Your Honor. There was an emergency with my mother," I lie. Quickly ending the call, I place my phone back on the table.

I realize my mistake as soon as his angry expression turns to one of concern.

"If you need to take a recess, Counselor, speak up now."

How did it completely slip my mind that Judge Robertson knows my parents? My father plays golf with Judge Robertson once a week. I don't make mistakes like this. Ever. The only explanation for my carelessness is that there's been a lot going on. My brain is being forced into a hundred different directions.

"It's fine, Your Honor. We can proceed."

While the defense continues with their arguments, I jot myself a note at the top of my yellow legal pad to pick up the subpoena and to let my father know that if Judge Robertson asks how mother is, he should just go along with it.

The likeliness of that happening is zero to none, though. My father is an Indiana Supreme Court judge and my mother teaches advanced criminal law at Notre Dame. They have no tolerance for frivolity and would never understand if I told them I was interrupted in court by a phone call from one of my friends.

Bzzzzzzzzz.

The sound of my cell phone bouncing across the table again forces me out of my depressing thoughts.

I swear to God I'm going to kill Paige.

With a quick smack of my hand on top of it, I silence the noise. I glance nervously up at Judge Robertson to see if he heard it. Luckily, he's called the defense up to his bench and they are deep in conversation.

"Paige, I swear, someone better be dead." I give an apologetic smile to my client seated next to me.

"Yes! Yes! Oh, God! Oh, Matt! Harder!"

My eyes widen in horror and I quickly end the call.

Did she really just call me while she was having sex?

This time, I remember to power my cell phone down and shove it quickly into my purse on the floor. No wonder I'm so distracted. I've had to deal with my two best friends falling in love right in front of my eyes after we all swore off men for the rest of our lives.

My parents don't know this yet, but I'm part owner of the company we opened together—Fool Me Once Investigations. It was the first time in my life I was actually excited about something. I've been putting off sharing this news with them for months. Since my sham of a marriage to Doug ended, I've felt lost. Felt as if I'm floundering around from day to day trying to figure out my life and what makes me happy. Doug certainly found his happiness—with another man.

Maybe that's why I've been slow to inform my parents. Once they know what I've been doing in my spare time, it will no longer be all mine. The choices I've made and the work I've been doing for Fool Me Once will be theirs to pick apart and criticize.

The remainder of the preliminary hearing goes off without a hitch. Judge Robertson decides that there is no probable cause for the complaint against my client and, thankfully, we won't be going to trial.

Rushing out of the courtroom, I pull my cell phone out of my purse, power it back up, and call Paige.

She answers on the first ring. "Please don't kill me. I'm so sorry for calling you during court. I swear it won't happen again."

I sigh as I pull my rolling leather briefcase behind me and push through the double doors at the front of the courthouse, exiting into the sunshine.

"I'd rather you apologize for calling me when you and Matt were having sex," I deadpan.

Paige gasps in surprise and then starts laughing. "Oh, my God! I butt dialed you!"

She continues laughing and I can hear Matt laughing along with her through the line.

"Tell Matt he owes me a bottle of bleach to pour into my ears."

Paige and Matt met a month ago when one of Paige's cases for Fool Me Once required her to catch him cheating. She quickly found out he wasn't a cheater and that his ex was trying to take his father's company away from him in the divorce proceedings.

I'm happy for them, I really am. Just because I'm finished with love doesn't mean I can't celebrate when my best friends find it again.

"I picked up the subpoena for Richard Covington from the court administrator and I'm heading over to his place now," I tell her as I unlock my Mercedes, lower the handle of my bag, and lift it into the passenger seat.

We were hired by another law firm to deliver the subpoena to Richard. Since I'm the one who works at the courthouse, it was a given that I'd be in charge of this job.

"All right, good luck with that. I've seen pictures of him in *Forbes*. That man is hot as hell. Don't fall victim to his good looks and charm," Paige teases.

Like that would ever happen. First of all, Richard Covington is still technically married. That's not something I would go near with a ten-foot pole. I've been married to a cheater who liked men. I'm not about to fall for a straight cheater in the middle of a vicious divorce battle. His ex is trying to take Mr. Wandering-Eye Moneybags for all he's got.

There isn't a man alive right now worth giving up my independence for.

"I'm pretty sure I'll be able to resist him, Paige," I tell her with a roll of my eyes as I start up my car. "This subpoena is asking him to turn over all records of his Internet usage. Men like him are too cocky to ever delete their Internet history."

"I bet he's got some kinky fetishes too. Oh, to be a fly on the wall when the divorce lawyers go through his computer," she says with a sigh.

"Seriously, Paige? You were just telling me how good-looking he was like you thought I should make a go for him. It's nice to know you have my best interests at heart," I say.

"Hey, kinky fetishes can be fun. Unless he's into barnyard animals."

I try not to gag at that mental image. "That's disgusting."

"You never know. It could just be some fun S&M or three-way action. He's hot enough for you to forgive a little proclivity like that," Paige tells me with a laugh.

"I'm hanging up now, Paige. This conversation has officially made its descent right into the gutter."

"Can I help it if I want you to find someone and be happy like I am?" she asks.

"I'm perfectly happy on my own. I told you that."

"Whatever helps you sleep at night, Lorelei. One of these days you're going to find a man who will change everything," she warns.

I sigh and wish she could see me shaking my head at her. "I already met the man who did that. He's now getting married to a waiter from my favorite Italian restaurant."

Even if I wanted to take a chance again, it's not like I have the time. My caseload for the firm is reaching epic proportions and I've been trying to handle more things at Fool Me Once so Kennedy and Paige can have more free time with the men in their lives.

"I'm not giving up on you, Lorelei. There's hope for you yet. Call me when you're finished with the subpoena. Matt has a meeting and

Kennedy mentioned something about us going out for drinks to discuss a few new cases that came in."

I end the call with a promise to call her back and toss my cell phone onto the passenger seat. I could use a girls' night out. I'm having dinner with my parents next weekend and I need some advice from my friends on whether or not it's time to come clean with them about Fool Me Once.

Thankfully, all that's involved with this subpoena is knocking on Richard Covington's door, having him verbally confirm his identity, and then handing over the document. I should be on my way to meet Kennedy and Paige within the hour.

CHAPTER 2

⌒

Twenty minutes later I pull into Breakwater Village, the gated community in the city of Granger, where Richard Covington lives. After I give my information to the guard at the gate, he takes down my license plate number and waves me through.

Due to my parents' careers, I grew up in a home that some might call a mansion among some of the wealthiest people in Indiana. Every weekend we attended one function or another at country clubs or the lavish homes of these friends. And with my law career, I'm used to being around people of wealth and stature and spending evenings in their large homes. But even I'm a little bit in shock as I pull into Richard Covington's circular driveway.

The house looming in front of me is a beautiful English manor situated on a large wooded lot with professionally landscaped shrubbery and flower gardens. Though it's large, it doesn't quite block the lake and boat dock behind it. I get out of my car and smooth my hands down the front of my Chanel suit, checking my reflection in the car window to make sure my shoulder-length straight brown hair is still in order.

My mother would have a field day if she knew I was walking up to Richard Covington's front door right now. She's been trying to get Richard to attend one of her charity events for years now. According to the *Forbes* magazine article that Paige referred to, he is the richest man in Indiana. His fortune, now in the billions, was made when he invented a medical device in his final year of med school.

Clutching the subpoena in my hand, I ring the doorbell and wait.

And then wait some more.

I parked behind a brand-new Cadillac in the driveway, so I'm assuming someone has to be here.

I ring the doorbell again and, after waiting another few minutes without an answer, I reach up and knock. The door pushes open as soon as my knuckles rap against the wood.

Looking nervously back over my shoulder first, I slowly poke my head through the doorway. "Mr. Covington?"

There's no response to my shout except for the tick of a clock in the entryway. Something doesn't feel right about this. My gut is telling me to leave and try again at another time. Unfortunately, my brain is reminding me that I should just suck it up, because this is what I want to do with my life. Not deliver subpoenas, per se, but detective work—something thrilling, challenging, and that actually makes me happy.

Deciding to listen to my brain like I always do, I take a tentative step into the house and try calling out again. "Mr. Covington? Hello? Is anyone home?"

I crane my neck around the door and listen quietly for any sounds of movement in the house. Although with a house this big, someone could be driving a dump truck through one of the rooms in the east wing and I wouldn't even hear it.

He must have hired help in a place this huge. It's hard to believe that even if he isn't home, someone else isn't in the house somewhere and wouldn't have heard the doorbell. Even in my parents' home, their housekeeper, Mrs. Cooper, is always there.

"HELLO?" I try again, louder than before.

My voice echoes around the massive cathedral ceiling in the entryway.

I finally decide to give up and try again another day. Regardless of whether or not the door was open, it's not a good idea for me to just walk into someone's house uninvited. Especially when I'm here to deliver them a court document that is most likely going to anger them. Plus, the quiet emptiness of this house is starting to unnerve me.

As I turn to leave, the loud screech of a hysterical cat shatters the silence. I scream in surprise and stumble back against the open door as a white Persian races by me, hissing and yowling as it goes. My eyes widen in shock when I see that it left little red paw prints in its wake.

Swallowing thickly, I step over the paw prints and look in the direction the cat came from. The red markings start in the next room to the left. Without even thinking, I head in that direction, my heels clicking loudly on the floor as I go. As I step into the room, the hardwood floor switches over to carpet and my heels sink into its plushness.

I'm in the library—full bookcases line every wall of the room. The rest of the décor loses my focus as my gaze narrows in on something completely out of place in this otherwise spotless home. The red paw prints I had been following lead right up to a body on the floor in the middle of the room. A body that is sprawled across the cream carpet with a bullet hole between its wide-open, lifeless eyes and a pool of blood soaking into the carpet under its head.

All the breath leaves my lungs with a whoosh when I see that the body in front of me is that of Richard Covington.

—◆—

"One more time, Lorelei. Tell me exactly what you saw when you walked into the library."

Kennedy's brother Ted was the first on the scene after I called the police, and he's been questioning me for the last half hour. I've gone over the details so many times now my brain feels like it's going to explode. While the medical examiner and a few detectives process the scene, Ted pulls me into the kitchen and away from the chaos to question me more.

"Here, drink this," Kennedy says as she holds a glass of amber liquid in front of me.

I reach for it without thinking and down it in one swallow, the burn of the alcohol making a fiery path down my throat and into my stomach. I cough and sputter as I slam the glass onto the counter in front of me.

"Where did you get that?" Ted demands.

Kennedy shrugs and takes a seat on one of the barstools next to me. "From the liquor cabinet in the living room."

"Goddammit, Kennedy! This is a crime scene. You can't just waltz around helping yourself to booze," Ted scolds.

"Oh, pipe down, asshole. Lorelei just saw her first dead body. The woman needed something to relax her."

Although I think I've been handling myself pretty well so far, I'm not going to pretend like I haven't felt a chill racing through my body ever since I found Richard shot dead in his library. Whatever Kennedy gave me tasted like gasoline and didn't go down very smoothly, but at least I don't feel cold anymore.

Ted sighs and shakes his head at his sister. Before he can reprimand her more, we hear greetings called to someone out in the foyer. Turning around in my chair, I realize Kennedy gave me that alcohol ten seconds too soon. My blood is now boiling at the sight of the person who is strolling into the kitchen.

"Hey, Dallas. Thanks for coming over," Ted says as Dallas walks up to him and they shake hands.

"No problem. I heard about it on my police scanner and was planning on heading over here anyway."

Dallas turns away from Ted and smirks at me. "Are you sure Lawyer here didn't shoot the guy?"

"Oh that's really mature," I fire back. I'm immediately disappointed in myself for letting him get to me.

It's no secret to anyone that Dallas Osborne and I don't exactly get along. He owns Osborne Investigations here in Granger, and Fool Me Once partners up with him every once in a while when we need backup on a case. We've known each other for about three months—three long months of hating the sight of each other.

A few weeks ago he helped Paige bring down one of the most notorious mob bosses in Indiana. One would think that since he helped out my friend and regularly helps out my company that I would be appreciative of him. Well, one would be wrong.

I might be more inclined to be nice to him if he wasn't such a Neanderthal and an arrogant jerk. It also doesn't help matters that he's entirely too good-looking and knows it—over six feet of pure muscle and brawn with tattoos up and down his strong arms, short, messy, dark brown hair, and light gray eyes.

"Is there any particular reason why he's here?" I ask Ted in annoyance.

"HE'S here because he was asked to be here," Dallas answers with smugness.

Ignoring him, I stare directly at Ted and wait for him to respond.

"There have been a bunch of budget cuts lately and we're shorthanded at the department. I asked Dallas to come over to see if he'd be willing to take on this case for us for the time being," Ted explains.

My hackles immediately go up and indignation runs through me. "Excuse me? I'm the one who was delivering the subpoena and found the body. If anyone is going to take on this case, it's going to be me."

Kennedy pats me on the back in a show of solidarity and I glare angrily at Dallas, refusing to back down on this.

"Lorelei, I would love to hand this entire thing over to you guys, but my hands are tied. You guys just don't have the right kind of experience for this sort of thing," Ted informs me.

"Oh, and Mr. Caveman over there *does?*"

My eyes still haven't left Dallas's, which means I get to see them light up when he smirks at me again.

Stupid man and his stupid smirk.

"Well, Lawyer, I used to be a police officer back in the day before I had to retire because of a knee injury. The department hired me to solve this case because of my invaluable knowledge. Which you are obviously lacking."

I grit my teeth and clench my hands into fists to avoid punching that mocking smile right off of his too-good-looking face.

I want this case. I want to find out who killed Richard Covington and prove to myself that this is something I could be really good at. The fact that Dallas can just waltz in here and take it right out of my hands makes me ill.

"If you want, I could let you help me out. I can always use someone to fetch me coffee and type up my notes," Dallas says.

Over my dead body.

"All right, Dallas, that's enough. I like you, but don't make me kick your ass," Kennedy warns him, coming to my defense.

What is it about this man that ties me up in knots? I've turned down hotter.

"Sorry, Kennedy. She just makes it so easy," Dallas says with a laugh.

Oh, that's right. He's a jerk.

"Dallas, if you want to follow me to the station, I'll make a copy of Lorelei's statement for you and also get you a copy of the

ME's findings," Ted tells him as he heads toward the door of the kitchen.

"I'll be right behind you in a few. I just want to check out the crime scene real quick," Dallas answers.

Ted nods. "Take your time. Ladies, I'll talk to you later. Lorelei, if you think of anything else, you can give me a call or just let Dallas know."

Yeah, like that's going to happen.

"You have my number. Feel free to call me anytime. I probably won't take your call though, because I'll be busy solving this case."

Dallas salutes Kennedy before sauntering out of the room. I'm appalled with myself that I stare at his firm backside until he disappears from sight.

"All right, now that they're gone, here's what you're going to do," Kennedy says, startling me out of my stare. "You're going to solve this fucking case and show Dallas Osborne where he can stick his Goddamn cockiness."

I sigh and shake my head at her. "You heard your brother. I can't work on this case because I'm not with the department."

"Since when do I ever listen to my brother? Fuck him and fuck Dallas. Seriously, you should really consider fucking Dallas. That man is *f-i-n-e*, fine. And he looks at you like he's picturing you naked."

I scoff at her and roll my eyes. "You're insane. He can't stand me. And obviously the feelings are mutual."

She raises one eyebrow. "Right. That's why you stared at his ass when he walked away."

I can feel my cheeks heat in embarrassment and I quickly look away from her.

Kennedy grabs my arm and pulls me off of my stool. "Come on, Paige is still waiting for us at the bar. We're going to suck back a few drinks and come up with a game plan."

I let Kennedy drag me through the house, making sure to keep my eyes straight ahead as we walk past the crime scene. Not just because I don't want another look at the dead body, but because Dallas is currently bent over said body. It's like his butt is trying to taunt me.

Sucking back a few drinks suddenly sounds like a great idea.

CHAPTER 3

"S o, what is this game plan you speak of?" I ask Kennedy and take a sip of my white wine spritzer.

I wait while she polishes off her glass of draft beer, wiping the back of her hand across her mouth as she sets the empty glass back down on the table with a thunk.

"The first part of the plan is that you need to stop ordering that girly shit every time we come to the bar. It's making us look bad."

Paige laughs and I shoot her a dirty look.

"How is what I drink making anyone look bad?"

Kennedy rests her elbows on the table and leans toward me. "If you want to make it in this business and get Dallas to take you seriously, you need to stop being so . . . boring."

I bristle at her comment and Paige reaches over to place her hand on top of my arm. "I think what Kennedy is trying to say is that you need to take some chances. Loosen up a little."

Kennedy shrugs and signals the bartender for another round. "Sure, what she said. I know you want to break out of this mold your parents have put you in, but you can't do that if you continue to do everything exactly the way they would. Drink some beer, curse like a sailor, and for God's sake, stop using fucking hand sanitizer."

I pause with the small bottle in my hand. "I could care less if Dallas Osborne takes me seriously. And really, Kennedy, do you have any idea what kind of germs are on this table?"

Kennedy rolls her eyes before dramatically thumping her head down on said table.

"The fact of the matter is, Dallas is in charge of this investigation now," Paige states. "If you want to get anywhere with this case, you're going to need to get into his head. Think like he would and do what he would do so you can be one step ahead of him."

I've played it safe for so long that I'm not even sure if I know how to do something like this, but I'm willing to give it a try. I'll do just about anything to solve this case, even if it means going to the dark side and getting in Dallas's disgusting, pigheaded brain. The only problem is, taking on this case means we won't get paid. If I do this instead of handling one of our other cases, money is going to be tight.

Kennedy lifts her head from the table. "Forget about the beer and the cursing for right now. The first part of this plan will be a piece of cake for you—research. Find everything and anything you can on the life and times of Richard Covington. And not just the typical stuff like who he was friends with and who had grudges against him. Even information like who he banged in high school and what his favorite foods were could be helpful. Dig up everything you can find and then start asking questions."

"Are you forgetting the fact that we're not being paid for this? And if Ted or Dallas finds out what I'm doing, I could get into serious trouble."

Not that I really care what Dallas thinks, but I don't want to shoot myself in the foot at the very beginning.

"Ted is too busy right now to worry about what you're doing. And seeing you go against your good-little-lawyer role will throw Dallas off his game. You'll be able to swoop in and save the day while he's sitting there with his dick in his hand."

I wince. I really didn't need that mental image in my brain.

"You could even negotiate with him that if you solve the case, you get the fee," Kennedy adds.

She makes it sound so easy. Being able to pay the electric bill next month relies on my solving a crime before Dallas.

"So, now that that's settled, can we move on to something vitally important?" Kennedy asks. "Griffin wants to take me away for the weekend in a few weeks. And I'm pretty sure he's going to propose."

An earsplitting scream leaves Paige's lips and she starts bouncing up and down in her chair.

Kennedy and I cringe until she finally calms down.

"Oh, my God! Are you serious? We have to go shopping!" Paige exclaims.

"How did I know you were going to say that?" Kennedy complains.

Paige pulls her cell phone out of her purse and clicks on the Internet icon. "We have to get you some sexy lingerie. I think there's a sale at Victoria's Secret tomorrow. How do you feel about spray tans?"

Kennedy's eyes widen in horror.

"Nothing drastic, just a dusting of color. We should also get your roots touched up. Are you thinking dress or skirt for the actual proposal? I'm thinking skirt with a nice pair of Gucci snakeskin knee boots," Paige continues, ignoring Kennedy's disgusted expression as she searches the Internet.

"If she forces me to go shopping, you're coming with me," Kennedy demands.

⌐●

A few hours later, I'm curled up on my couch with a fire in the fireplace, the file for this case and my laptop resting on the arm of the couch next to me.

I've always loved my home. My parents looked down their noses at it when I bought it, which probably convinced me even more that it was the perfect place for me. It's a small Cape Cod in a development full of nice middle-class families.

When I graduated from law school, it was assumed I would take a position at my father's firm in Indianapolis and continue living close to them. After being on my own for so many years at Harvard and finally being able to breathe without their constant interference in my life, I knew as soon as I received my degree that I couldn't go back there. It was my one and only form of rebellion. Much to my parents' dismay, I accepted an offer with a firm in South Bend, almost an hour and a half from where they live.

Unfortunately, it still wasn't far enough away to avoid their judgment and the hold they continue to have on my life.

I want them to finally understand that I am my own person and I need to do what makes me happy, not what makes them look good. The idea of taking on a murder case and actually solving it thrills and scares me all at the same time.

Settling back into the couch, I begin searching the Internet for more information on Richard. I'm going to need to find out a lot more about this man than what I've read in magazines. Not only do I need to look deeper into Richard's background, but also into everyone's background associated with him. From the articles I've read in the past, I know he was married to Stephanie, a woman thirty years his junior *(eew)*. The spouse—especially a soon-to-be ex—is always the first suspect.

Thinking back over what Kennedy told me, I realize it's inevitable that I'm going to need to get into Dallas's head. What would Dallas do in this instance? He would probably do something illegal like search through sealed court documents or break into the ex-wife's home.

I'm not ready to go to extremes like that. I'm smart and resourceful and I have tons of legal knowledge at my disposal. I can do this without stooping to his level. Pulling up PACER, the public-access website for court records, I type in Stephanie's name to see if she's ever had any trouble with the law or if Richard ever filed any complaints against her.

The ringing of my cell phone on the cushion next to me pulls my focus away from the screen of my laptop. Glancing at the display, I see that it's an unknown number. Figuring I need to answer it in case it's one of my clients calling from a different line, I grab the phone and bring it up to my ear.

"Lorelei Warner."

There's a snort on the other end of the line. "Wow, you even answer the phone all pretentious."

Clenching my teeth, I take a deep breath before answering. "What do you want, Dallas, and how did you get my number?"

"Awww, don't be like that, Lawyer. You know you've been waiting by the phone for my call," he tells me with a clear effort to sound sexy.

No. There is nothing about Dallas Osborne that's sexy.

"Sorry to bother you. I'm sure you're quite busy sitting at home on a Monday night, thinking about how much you hate the male species," he adds with a laugh.

"I'm hanging up now."

Pulling the phone away, I hear him shout through the line and I slowly bring it back up to my ear.

"Look, I don't like you and you don't like me. Can we call a truce for just one second?" Dallas asks with a sigh.

Waiting for him to continue, I don't say a word.

"I'm going over Ted's notes from your statement and I can't read a damn word of his chicken-scratch handwriting. I just need to know whether or not you noticed the front door had been tampered with when you entered Richard Covington's house," he explains.

He wants my assistance with the case that should have been mine. This jerk actually thinks I'm going to help him?

"You're absolutely correct. It *would* probably be the best thing for this case if we put our differences aside. After all, the goal right now is to find out who did this."

I hear Dallas sigh in relief. "Exactly. It's good that you can be the bigger person about this, Lorelei."

Hearing my name fall from his lips gives me pause. He's never said my name before, just variations of insults. I ignore the tug on my heart that it gives me and remember Kennedy's words: shock him so much that it will throw him off his game.

"Oh, I'm definitely the bigger person in this instance, Dallas," I tell him sweetly. "Grab a pen and jot this down."

I can hear him rustling around through the line.

"I'm ready. Go."

Channeling Kennedy, I toss aside my uptight nature for just a moment. "I'm going to wipe your ass with this case, Dallas Osborne. When I find out who killed Richard Covington, and I will, I'm going to point and laugh while you're busy sitting at home on a Monday night with your dick in your hand."

Ending the call, I toss my phone onto my coffee table and smile to myself.

Getting inside Dallas's head might just be the best advice Kennedy has ever given me.

CHAPTER 4

"I don't know why I'm even shocked that you carry tools with you for breaking and entering," I tell Kennedy as I watch her crouch down in front of Richard Covington's door.

It's been a week since I walked in this house to find Richard shot dead on the floor of his library. I had two cases to try and spent the rest of my time pulling up as much information as I could find on Richard and Stephanie. I probably never should have told Kennedy that I wished I could have an hour inside of Richard's house to see if I could find anything that would help with the case. An hour later she knocked on my door and told me to wear black and bring a flashlight.

"I can't believe we're doing this. You know I could be disbarred for this, right?" I complain to Kennedy as I turn my back on her and stare out over the dark lawn. If I'm not watching it happen, I can just plead ignorance if we get caught.

"I thought you were going to quit. Who cares if they fire you?" Paige whispers as she aims her flashlight at the door so Kennedy can see.

"There's a big difference between being fired and being disbarred, Paige. If we get caught, I could lose my license and never be able to practice law again."

I should really be more concerned about the ramifications of what we're doing right now. I shouldn't be standing here while my friend breaks into a crime scene. At least one problem would be solved—my parents would finally know what I've been doing when they have to bail me out of jail.

"First rule of thumb if you're going to make it in this business, Lorelei: always carry a paper clip and a torsion wrench in your back pocket and stop being such a candy ass," Kennedy explains as she carefully sticks the tools into the lock with the precision of a surgeon performing open-heart surgery.

"I thought the first rule of thumb was to stick it to the man?" Paige says with a laugh.

"What the hell are we going to do if the alarm goes off?" I whisper, glancing behind us nervously.

"The alarm isn't going to go off because Ted told me they had it disabled for the next few days so detectives can come and go whenever they please," Kennedy says, her eyes never leaving the door as she fiddles with the lock.

A few seconds later, I hear a loud click.

"Got it!" Kennedy cheers.

She pulls another tool out of her back pocket, this time a Swiss Army knife, and slices through the police tape stretched across the door. She stands up, pushes open the door, and we follow her into the dark house.

"I'll replace that when we leave. Keep your flashlights low to the ground. We don't want anyone driving by to see the light bouncing around through the windows," Kennedy warns.

We all turn on our flashlights and aim them at the ground.

"You're sure the guard at the front gate won't tell anyone we were here?" I ask her nervously as we step into the foyer.

"Positive. I went to high school with the guy and a few months ago his ex-wife had me confront him about wearing her underwear and heels. I told him I would send out a mass e-mail to everyone he knows," Kennedy tells us.

"Oh, my God, *that* was the guy who pranced around his kitchen in fishnets and stilettos?" Paige asks in shock as I close the door behind us.

Kennedy nods as she shines her flashlight from left to right. "That's him. The ex came home early from work to see him doing the entire final dance sequence from *Dirty Dancing*."

Paige and I stand behind Kennedy while she looks around and decides which direction to head.

"This place is really creepy. Someone died here," Paige complains quietly as we inch slowly through the foyer and toward the library.

Even though it's dark and Kennedy has her back to us, I can tell she's rolling her eyes. "Oh, stop being such a baby. It's not like his body is still in here."

"You can't tell me this doesn't freak you out a little bit. You just stepped over the exact spot where his body was. That's just gross," Paige says with a shiver as we all walk around the bloodstain on the cream carpet.

Kennedy ignores her and makes her way over to the giant oak desk on the far side of the room. "I'll start with this room. Lorelei, you check the rest of the first floor. This dude has a house the size of a small country. He could have ten offices in a house this large, but instead, he uses the library right on the ground floor. Obviously he's weird. Paige, you can start going room to room upstairs and see if you can find any other file cabinets or some place where Richard would keep paperwork. He's got to have a safe in this house—see if you guys can find that too."

"Why the hell do I have to be the one to wander through the upstairs by myself?"

Paige stands by the doorway with her arms wrapped around herself.

"There is nothing to be afraid of. It's just an empty house. Suck it up and get to work," Kennedy tells her. "Maybe if you're lucky, you'll come across the ex's closet. She moved out a while ago, but I heard the officers talking the other day when we were here that she left some things behind."

Even with just the faint beams of our flashlights I can see Paige's eyes light up with excitement.

"If you need me, I'll be upstairs."

She turns and races out of the room and a few seconds later I hear her feet pounding up the stairs quickly.

For the next twenty minutes, I stroll from room to room downstairs, not finding anything of any interest. I make my way back to the library and see that Kennedy has pulled out all the files from the desk and is reading through them.

"I can't believe Paige was creeped out coming in this house," Kennedy says with a laugh when she sees me walk in. "She is the biggest puss—SON OF A FUCKING BITCH, WHAT THE HELL WAS THAT?"

The uncharacteristic girly scream from Kennedy has me racing over to her. I watch as she jumps up on the chair behind the desk, whipping her hand with the flashlight back and forth under the desk.

"Something touched my leg! SOMETHING TOUCHED MY FUCKING LEG!" she screams.

Aiming my flashlight under the desk, I walk slowly around it until I'm right next to Kennedy's chair.

"I don't see anything. Are you sure you didn't just bump up against the desk?" I ask as I crouch down to get a better look.

"I didn't bump against the Goddamn desk! Something reached out and smacked my ankle," she argues angrily.

I try to hide my amusement at how upset Kennedy is right now.

"What were you saying to Paige a few seconds ago?" I ask as I continue my way around the massive desk. "Stop being such a baby?"

I can't contain a snort of laughter.

"Don't make me come down off of this chair and kick your ass, Lorelei."

I laugh again and shake my head at her. "There's nothing here. I think you just—OH, MY GOD, WHAT IS THAT?!"

Something that sounds like a cross between a rattlesnake and a dying person keens from under the desk. I scramble away from it, tripping over my feet and landing on my butt. My flashlight falls from my hand and rolls across the floor, the beam flashing around the room like a strobe light.

"I told you! I told you something touched me!" Kennedy yells in victory.

I continue scooting backward, as far away from the desk as possible. "Stop sounding so excited that something is under that desk trying to kill us!"

Suddenly, the room is bathed in bright light and I wince, blinking my eyes rapidly to adjust to it.

"Turn off the light! What if someone sees it?" Kennedy yells at Paige, who stands in the doorway.

With a roll of her eyes, Paige stalks across the room then gets down on her hands and knees, the top half of her body disappearing under the desk. The hissing and moaning gets louder when Paige suddenly pops back out from under the desk with a white ball of angry cat in her hands.

"Seriously? I could hear you screaming all the way upstairs. The neighbors probably heard you. Having a light on is the least of your worries," Paige complains as she stands up with the cat firmly grasped by the back of its neck.

After getting up from the floor, I walk over to the cat.

"Awww, you poor thing. You've been alone in this house for a week. She still has dried blood on her paws."

The cat answers my concern for her by hissing with so much force that spit flies from her mouth.

"While you two idiots were freaking out over a cat, I found some interesting e-mails in a drawer in Richard's room," Paige tells us, handing the cat over to me and then bending down to pick up a few pieces of paper that she set down on the floor when she crawled under the desk.

The cat looks up at me with big, sad eyes and right when I feel like we have a connection, she starts the low growl in her throat all over again and hisses at me.

Kennedy hops down from the chair and I turn to hand the cat off to her.

She immediately puts her hands up in the air and shakes her head. "Oh no. Don't even think about it. That cat is an asshole."

The cat hisses and tries to lunge out of my arms for Kennedy. I grip her as hard as I can to keep her from ripping Kennedy's face off.

"Don't call her that," I whisper. "Obviously she's traumatized from watching her owner get killed."

I hold on to her with one arm and try to calm her down by scratching her behind the ears.

Kennedy takes a step forward and glares at the cat. "Not so tough now, are you?"

The cat growls and I turn away from Kennedy so she'll stop taunting her.

"So, what are these e-mails you found in Richard's room?" I ask Paige.

She holds out the pieces of paper and Kennedy takes them from her and glances over them.

"Well, well, well. It looks like Richard's lawyer was trying to blackmail him," Kennedy says with a smile. "A month ago he sent Richard an e-mail telling him that if Richard didn't give him a quarter of a million dollars, he would tell everyone what he knows."

"Does it say what he knew?" I ask.

Kennedy flips through the pages. "Nope. They go back and forth a few times and Richard basically tells him to fuck off."

Kennedy hands the papers over to me, and when I see the name and e-mail address at the top of the page, my mouth drops open. "Oh, my God. I know this guy. I went to law school with him."

Miles Harper. He was in my graduating class and I had a few study groups with him. He was a jerk then and the few times I've seen him at social functions since law school have only proved he hadn't changed a bit.

"Well, then, getting him to talk to you should be a piece of cake," Paige tells me with a smile.

"Paige, why do you have on sparkly silver shoes?" Kennedy suddenly asks.

I look down at Paige's feet and sure enough, the black boots she wore here have been replaced with a pair of four-inch stilettos covered in crystals.

"Did you really think I would find the closet of a billionaire's ex-wife and NOT try on a pair of her shoes? I can't believe she left these behind."

Paige twists and turns her foot so that the light sparkles off of her footwear.

"The shoes stay here," Kennedy warns her.

Paige stomps her stilettoed foot. "But she doesn't even want them! And she's got six pairs just like them. These are from Daniele Michetti's Summer 2010 collection. It's Swarovski!"

"What are you, Russian?" Kennedy complains. "I have no idea what you're saying to me."

The cat growls at Kennedy.

"Oh, pipe the fuck down, cat. Put the shoes back and let's get the hell out of here."

Kennedy grabs my flashlight off of the ground and follows

Paige as she stomps out of the room to put the shoes back. Kennedy pauses by the door and looks back at me when she realizes I'm not following her.

I resist the question in her gaze, giving her my best pout, and I pet the cat's head. Finally, she throws her hands up in the air. "Oh, you have got to be kidding me."

I huff. "Kennedy, I can't just leave her here. She's dirty and hungry and all alone."

Kennedy shakes her head at me and sighs. "Fine. But if that thing so much as looks at me funny on the ride home, I'm opening the car door and shoving you both out into oncoming traffic."

CHAPTER 5

$\backsim\!\!\backsim$

After we got home from searching Richard's house a few nights ago, I fed Snowball a can of tuna and attempted to give her a bath. I still have scratches up and down my arms and the wet cat didn't come out from under my bed for a full day. Even dry, she still chooses to hide under there, hissing and growling at me all night long, every single night.

I'm now thinking the name Snowball isn't very fitting for her.

In between research on Richard Covington and trying to coax the cat out from under my bed without injury, I looked up what I could find on Miles Harper in our alumni directory. It turns out he's practicing law at my father's old firm. Since I'm having dinner with my parents this weekend, I figured I'd wait until I'm out that way to try and talk to him.

In the meantime, I decided it was time to start questioning a few people. For the most part, Richard Covington led a pretty normal life. He was raised in an upper-class family, he had no siblings, and there aren't any living relatives left. He went to school to be a doctor, invented a new type of mechanism for heart catheters, and made billions. He met his wife a few years ago while he was giving a speech at his alma mater. She was a student there, of course. Why should a fifty-five-year-old billionaire marry someone his own age?

According to all of the research I've done so far, he was an upstanding citizen and a philanthropist, giving to as many charities as he could. His only downfall was his addiction to porn. Or so said his ex-wife's Facebook page. The majority of her status messages ever since they separated were along the lines of, "I struggled with this for so long, but it's finally time to come clean. Richard and I separated because of his addiction to porn."

I am so glad I didn't grow up in the land of Facebook. Nothing like airing your dirty laundry for the entire world to see. This just makes her even more of a suspect now in my book.

Since I don't want anyone knowing what I'm up to, I'm using a fake name and fake reason for all of the questions. I decided a good place to start would be the ex.

"Hello, Mrs. Covington, I'm Lori Wagner. We spoke on the phone the other day?"

Stephanie Covington stands in the doorway of her condo with a cup of tea in her hand and looks at me in confusion for a few moments.

"Oh, that's right. You're the reporter," she says as she nods, holding the door wider. "Come in; I was just making taheebo tea. My herbalist told me I have a sluggish liver. Would you like a cup? Do you have a sluggish liver?"

I have no idea how to respond to this, so I just smile and politely decline as I walk through the doorway.

Stephanie Covington isn't at all what I pictured when I found out she was thirty years younger than her husband. Well, looks-wise she fits that picture to a T. She's twenty-five years old and super-model gorgeous with long blond hair and a chest that has had some help, judging by the way she's practically spilling out of her skin-tight red dress.

But to be honest, I imagined she would behave like an elitist, gold-digging child. But when we spoke on the phone, Stephanie was more than happy to answer some of my questions and was extremely polite.

"You'll have to excuse the mess. I've just been too depressed since I heard about Richard to even think about having the maid come by," Stephanie explains.

I glance around and briefly wonder what this woman thinks is a "mess." The place is pretty spotless from where I stand.

"I'm so sorry for your loss, Mrs. Covington. As I said on the phone, I just need to ask you a few questions."

She sits down on the love seat in the sitting room and gestures for me to take a seat across from her on the matching couch.

"Please, call me Stephanie." She leans over the arm of the love seat and pulls a tissue out of a box, dabbing gently under her eyes. "It's still such a shock. We had our differences and the divorce wasn't going very smoothly, but he was still my husband, and I loved him when we married."

I smile softly at her and give her time to compose herself.

"If you don't mind me asking, Stephanie, why were you and Mr. Covington separating?"

Aside from the porn addiction.

She sighs and folds her hands in her lap. "It's the same old story. A few years after we got married, he decided to turn me in for a younger model. I caught him screwing his secretary on his desk. I had decided to surprise him with dinner when he was supposed to be working late."

Even though I feel bad for Stephanie, she just made herself a prime suspect.

As if reading my mind, she continues. "I know what you're thinking. I know what *everyone* is thinking. I killed him in a jealous rage. But Richard and I had been having problems even before I caught him cheating. To put it delicately, Richard had a fondness for pornographic movies. And I'm not just talking a few viewings here and there. I mean, he watched it all the time. Morning, noon, and night. He even took it to the office. I begged him to get help, but he just laughed it off. I told him I would leave him if he didn't stop and the next thing I know, I'm walking in on him reenacting a scene with another woman. People think I might have killed him because he was trying to stiff me in the divorce. But Richard was worth more alive than he is dead."

I look at her in confusion. "I'm sorry; I don't follow."

"My dearly departed ex didn't believe in life insurance. He was fifty-five years old and he refused to go to the doctor even for a checkup. And now that he's gone, his board of directors will take over the shares of his company, because even though he didn't believe in protecting his life, he made damn sure to protect the only thing he ever loved," she says bitterly.

Well, there goes that idea.

"Do you know anyone who might have had a grudge against your husband? A business associate or a friend whom he might have wronged?"

"I went over all of this with the detective who stopped by yesterday. Dallas, I think he said his name was. He was so nice—he took me out for drinks," Stephanie says with a sniffle.

Oh, I'm sure Dallas was very nice at helping you forget by trying to get in your pants.

"Anyway, I just realized that I forgot to tell him last night that he should also question Richard's old business partner, Andrew Jameson," Stephanie tells me, crossing her legs and leaning back against the love seat.

Well, at least one good thing came from Dallas being a man whore last night: he was so busy feeding her alcohol and making her "forget," that I know something he doesn't.

"I don't know everything that happened between them, but I know that they didn't part on the best of terms when Andrew decided to leave the company. Are you going to put all of this in the article you're writing? I don't want Andrew to know I'm pointing fingers at him or anything."

Oops, the article!

"Um, no, don't worry about that at all. I'll make sure to keep your name out of it," I lie.

Stephanie looks relieved at my answer and continues. "I don't know how many times I heard Richard on the phone with Andrew arguing. Richard was offering him quite a lot of money to buy him out, but Andrew felt like it wasn't enough. Their arguments were just horrendous. They disrupted my chakras and I just couldn't seem to get my life force back on track after that. My herbalist had to cleanse my aura three times a week just so I could sleep."

Oh, my God.

I don't want to seem rude, but I need to get out of here right away and get to this Andrew Jameson's house before Dallas finds out about him. Or before Stephanie wants to cleanse my chakras.

"Stephanie, I appreciate you taking the time to speak with me today. I have a prior appointment I need to get to. Would it be okay just to chat on the phone if I have any more questions?" I ask as I rise from the couch.

She walks me to the door. "Absolutely. I'll do anything I can to help Richard's killer be brought to justice. If you don't mind my saying, you seem to have a very gray aura about you, Lori. That usually means you're troubled by something or you have deep secrets. People with gray auras are usually struggling to find balance."

Seriously? Is this a joke?

"I'm going to have my herbalist put something together for you. In the meantime, the best cure for a gray aura is love. You should get some love in your life, Lori."

I thank her without laughing and as she closes the door behind me, I wonder what color *her* aura is. Is there a color for mentally insane?

Rushing down the stairs, I see a 1965 black Mustang pull into the circular drive and park a few feet behind my car. I'm instantly filled with longing when I see it. I always wanted a car like that when I was a teenager, but my father thought it was impractical. There was a girl in my high school who had a car just like it. She was wild and fun and I wanted to be just like her.

I stop in my tracks and groan when I see who steps out of it. Of course *he* would own my dream car.

"Well, fancy seeing you here, Lawyer," Dallas says with a smirk as he saunters around the front of the car and walks up to me. "Are you having fun speaking to someone I already questioned?"

Folding my arms in front of me, I glare at him. "Questioned? Is that what they're calling it nowadays? Did you come back today to apologize to the widow for getting her drunk and taking advantage of her?"

Dallas leans in close to me. I can feel his breath on my face and see tiny specks of blue in his gray eyes. My heart rate picks up when he leans down and his cheek brushes against my own, and I wonder if he's going to whisper a secret in my ear. He smells like soap and there's a tiny hint of cologne mixed in that makes me feel warm all over.

"Careful there, Lawyer." His lips graze my ear when he speaks quietly. "You almost sound jealous."

I let out the breath I was holding when he moved in so close to me, noticing he didn't correct me when I accused him of taking advantage of Stephanie. Taking a step back to gather my wits, I roll my eyes at him. The heat I felt from moments ago disappears into thin air when I see the cocky smile on his face and realize he probably did sleep with her to get the answers to his questions.

"You're delusional."

"And you're in over your head. You can't handle this case. Go back to your courtroom and stop trying to be something you're not," he informs me.

I'm so tired of people assuming they know what I can and can't handle. All people see when they look at me are three-piece suits and a brain, not someone who can solve a murder and kick Dallas Osborne's arrogant behind.

"You have no idea what I'm capable of, you smug bastard."

Shouldering past him, I make it to my car and slam the door closed behind me. I let myself fall apart just a little when I see that Dallas is no longer watching me and is already ringing the doorbell. My hands shake and I swallow past the lump in my throat. All my life someone has been trying to tell me what to do and I'm sick and tired of it. First my parents and now Dallas. I'm tired of being the woman who does as she's told. And on top of all that, now I have to worry about Dallas informing Ted that I was impersonating someone from the media to get close to a suspect.

Pulling my cell phone out of my purse, I make a call to my secretary at the law firm.

"Candace, I need you to pull up a case the firm handled about ten years ago for the Bay Corporation. I need an address for one of the members of the class-action lawsuit. His name is Andrew Jameson."

As I wait on the line for Candace to search through the archives on the computer, I try not to think about the fact that I'm doing something illegal right now that could compromise everything I've worked for over the last seventeen years. I'm crossing a line.

Candace gets back on the phone and tells me she'll have to call me back because it's going to take her a while to find the file, which ends up being perfect.

My next call is to Paige. Right now, her help is equally important.

"I'm coming over. I need to borrow some clothes."

I ignore her squeal of delight through the phone line and remind myself that I'm doing what I need to do to make it as a private investigator.

Hopefully I don't regret it.

CHAPTER 6

W ill you hold still? I can't get the eyeliner on right if you keep moving," Paige complains as she comes at me again with the black eye pencil.

"Is all of this really necessary? I just wanted to borrow some jeans and a T-shirt," I complain.

Paige ignores me and finishes up with my eye, taking a step back to admire her work.

"Dallas is going to be eating out of your hand when he sees you in this."

I roll my eyes at her and stand up from the edge of her bed, making my way over to the full-length mirror hanging behind her door. "Is he a horse? I don't want Dallas eating out of my hand. I couldn't care less if I ever see that jerk again."

"Yeah, good luck with that. I thought the same thing about Matt before I first met him," Paige replies with a smile.

I pause in front of the mirror and my jaw drops open.

"It's okay; you don't have to thank me. The look on your face is payment enough. You should go to dinner at your parents' house looking like this. Maybe then they'll take you seriously about not wanting to be a lawyer anymore."

I couldn't even speak if I wanted to. I look like Kennedy—like I could beat up a stranger in the street and not give it a second thought. Since Paige and I are roughly the same height, her skinny

Seven jeans fit me like a glove. She gave me a pair of knee-high black Gucci boots with silver buckles on the side, a white low-cut T-shirt, and a body-hugging black leather jacket.

My normally poker-straight brown hair has been curled into gentle waves that frame my face and the smoky eye makeup she artfully applied makes my boring brown eyes pop.

The best part is, I don't feel like a fraud in this outfit. I feel confident and sexy and like I could take on the world. And by the world, I mean my parents.

"Could you imagine if I showed up to dinner in this? They would have a heart attack," I whisper.

"Now all you need are a few tats and a nose piercing," Paige jokes.

My cheeks immediately redden at her words. A few weeks ago in a moment of complete self-pity and defiance, I got my first tattoo. I didn't tell anyone, not even my best friends. I was driving home from the courthouse, exhausted and frustrated after a phone call with my father where once again he had asked me what I had done so wrong that the firm hadn't announced me as partner yet.

The red neon sign for a tattoo shop caught my eye at a red light. When the light turned green, I stepped on the gas, cut across three lanes of traffic, and rushed inside.

It's Paige's turn to stare at me with her eyes wide and her mouth dropped open. "Oh, my God. Lorelei Warner, did you get a tattoo?"

My cell phone beeps loudly on Paige's side table and I rush over to grab it, rescuing myself from having to explain. It's a message from Candace with the address for Andrew Jameson.

"I have to go. I just got the address I was waiting for," I tell Paige as I shove my cell phone into my bag. Before I walk out the door, I quickly grab on to her and give her a hug.

"Thank you for this," I tell her softly before pulling away.

"It's just a little makeup and different clothes. It won't solve this case for you, but it sure as hell will give you some confidence. You look hot. And if you see Dallas, tell him to suck it," she says with a laugh.

Dallas makes me feel small and insignificant, just like my parents. I don't care how much he makes my insides flutter—if I never see him again, it will be too soon.

Paige's voice stops me as I reach her front door. "Oh, and Lorelei, you better tell me all about this tattoo when you're finished."

Double-checking the address in Candace's text and the location on my GPS, I stare at the house I'm parked in front of.

This can't be the right place. Andrew Jameson was the CEO of Richard's company. This house, if you can call it that, has boarded-up windows, a lawn that hasn't been mowed in years, and pieces of blue tarp covering holes in the roof. I reach over to my glove compartment and pull out my Taser, checking to make sure it's fully charged.

As I step out of my car, I glance around nervously at the neighborhood. I should have borrowed another vehicle to come here. My Mercedes sticks out like a sore thumb and I'm hoping it will be okay and still parked here when I come back outside.

I make my way up the rickety front porch steps and I forget about my car and just hope *I'll* be okay when I come back outside.

Knocking on the door, I quickly stash the Taser in my back pocket. This isn't the best neighborhood, but Andrew lives here and if I want him to answer my questions, I don't want to offend him right off the bat by showing him I'm carrying a weapon out of nervousness.

The door swings open and a man wearing ripped jeans and a stained sweatshirt stands there glaring at me. His hair is greasy and he's got the facial hair of a mountain man. This does not look like the former CEO of a multi-billion-dollar company.

"Andrew Jameson?"

The man grunts and brings a can of beer up to his mouth, taking a swig before belching with abandon.

"Who wants to know?"

I clear my throat and remind myself that I'm dressed to kill and get to the bottom of things. I stand up taller and take a deep breath.

"My name is Lori Wagner. I'm writing an article on the recent death of Richard Covington. I understand the two of you were friends and that you used to work together. Do you have a few minutes to answer some questions?"

Andrew crushes his empty beer can and tosses it somewhere behind him. "We were never friends. And as far as I'm concerned, that asshole got what was coming to him. I was there from day one. I helped him develop that fucking heart catheter tool, and after he marries that whore, he suddenly decides he doesn't need me anymore. Every idea I ever came up with while I worked for him, Richard got the credit for. And it was okay with me at the time; I was making good money. Thirty years of my life and all my good ideas I gave him and what's the thanks I get? A twenty-thousand-dollar severance package. I told him he could take his money and shove it up his ass."

Well, no wonder he's living in a hovel. It looks like he hasn't showered in months. Was his anger with Richard Covington enough to make him commit murder?

"Do you have any idea who could have killed him?" I ask, fishing for answers. I'm sure it's not going to be as easy as this guy coming right out and confessing, but you never know.

"I didn't kill him, if that's what you're asking. I hated that lying sack of shit, but I'm not a murderer. Richard wanted me out of the way because I knew all of his little secrets. You want to know who killed Richard Covington? Ask his—"

Andrew's voice is cut off by erupting gunshots. I feel a pain in my cheek like someone sliced it with a knife and watch Andrew's eyes widen in shock. My instincts kick into high gear and I immediately dive forward, slamming into Andrew and crashing to the ground on top of him in the doorway. More shots are fired, blowing out all of his windows. Shards of glass and slivers of wood from bullets slamming into the doorframe are raining down on top of us. I roll off of him, and with my head low, crawl as quickly as I can into the house. I glance behind me to make sure Andrew is following and see him still lying in the doorway.

"ANDREW! MOVE!" I scream as I scurry behind the couch and press my back up against it. I reach into my coat pocket for my cell phone and realize I left it back in my car.

After what feels like an eternity, the sound of gunfire stops. I slowly poke my head out from behind the couch and see that Andrew still hasn't moved. I feel something sticky and wet on the front of me and when I glance down, I see that Paige's white shirt is covered in blood. Since I'm pretty sure that blood isn't mine, I know I need to go over and check on Andrew. Swallowing my nausea down, I get back on my hands and knees and inch my way toward him, holding my breath and listening for the sound of a gun going off again.

Right now, all I hear is a ringing in my ears from the gunshots, and my heart thudding loudly. As I get closer to him, I feel shards of glass slicing into my palms and knees, but I ignore the pain. All I'm focused on is the man lying on his back staring up at the ceiling.

Please, not again. I can't handle two dead bodies in one week.

I eventually make it to Andrew's side and the first thing I see are several bullet holes in his chest. His sweatshirt is now not only stained with beer and food but his blood as well. It seeps out of the holes in his chest and blooms on the sweatshirt in one giant bloodred circle.

With a shaking hand, I reach out and press two fingers against the side of his neck. I wait for the beat of his heart against my fingers, but nothing happens.

Realizing that my fingers are pressed up against the neck of a dead body, I snatch my hand away and scramble backward until my shoulder hits the wall. Pulling my knees up to my chest, I wrap my arms around them and stare unblinking at the man I was just talking to moments ago.

Someone shot him. Someone shot at *me*. He was getting ready to tell me something important and was cut off by bullets to the chest before he could finish his sentence. Someone out there must have been following me and they didn't want Andrew to talk.

This is not good. Not good at all.

CHAPTER 7

L orelei. Come on, snap out of it, baby. Look at me."
The voice registers in my brain but it doesn't make sense. That voice wouldn't be talking to me this nicely. He'd also never call me "baby."

I feel warm hands on my face and my head is turned so I'm no longer staring at Andrew Jameson's dead body. Now I'm staring at a well-muscled chest in a tight blue shirt. My eyes slowly travel up and I see Dallas staring at me with a worried expression, his thumb wiping away at something on my cheek.

"Jesus Christ, you're bleeding. Breathe, Lorelei."

At his command, I let out a shaky breath and suddenly feel tears pooling in my eyes. I blink rapidly, refusing to let them fall. I don't know what Dallas is doing here or why he's being so nice to me, but I will absolutely not fall apart in front of him. That will only give him more ammunition.

Glancing around, I realize it's gotten dark. The sun was setting when I pulled up to Andrew's house. I must have been sitting here for a while. I remember sitting against the wall, afraid to go outside in case the shooter was still out there.

Everything comes rushing back at once. Talking to Andrew, a few seconds away from him telling me who killed Richard, and then gunshots. I wasn't even scared at the time—I must have been moving on pure adrenaline. But now the breaths are leaving my lungs quickly. Too quickly. I feel like I'm going to hyperventilate.

Dallas turns my face back to him and bends his head lower so he's looking directly in my eyes. "Don't look over there. Just look at me. It's okay. Nice and slow."

Nice and slow. In and out. Don't think about the fact that there's another dead body just a few feet away from me or that Dallas has the most amazing gray eyes I've ever seen and they're currently looking at me with gentle concern instead of irritation.

Dallas slides his hands off of my cheeks and I immediately miss their warmth. He reaches down and grabs both of my wrists, pulling my hands up and inspecting them.

"Fuck. Your hands are full of glass," he curses as he gently starts plucking a few pieces out.

I look down and realize he's right. I stare unblinking at the palms of my hands. They are covered in dots of blood and tiny shards of glass and they suddenly hurt like hell.

He lets go of one of my hands and quickly reaches into his back pocket, pulling out a handkerchief. He brings it up to the side of my face and presses it against my cheek. I flinch when it touches my skin and feel a small sting of pain.

"It's all right—it's just a small scratch. A bullet must have grazed you," he says calmly.

The look on his face contradicts the softness in his tone. He's clenching his teeth and a muscle ticks in his jaw. He's probably angry with me that I came in here, acting like I knew what I was doing, and now a prime suspect is dead.

I want to defend myself, but I can't make the words form. What if it was my fault? Maybe someone saw me leaving Stephanie's house and they followed me here. What if I'm the reason Andrew Jameson is dead?

The distant sound of sirens pulls Dallas's gaze away from mine and he quickly looks out the open door and then back to me.

"Hurry, get up."

He grabs my arms and pulls me to my feet.

"The cops are going to be all over this place in ten minutes. You need to get the fuck out of here," he tells me, pulling me toward the door.

"What? What are you talking about? I can't leave," I tell him, finally finding my voice and planting my feet firmly in place, refusing to move. "I just saw a man shot to death. A man that I was questioning in a murder investigation. I need to tell the police what happened."

Dallas huffs in irritation, clenching my arm and trying to pull me closer to the door. Even though I'm a little confused by the careful way he handled me moments ago, it doesn't escape my notice that right now all he cares about is getting me out of here. Judging by all of our interactions since we met, there's only one possible explanation for his need to shove me out the door before anyone sees me.

"You just want the stupid glory all for yourself. I hate to break it to you, but I'M the one who found out about Andrew Jameson, not you. I got here first and you can't stand that, can you?" I fire at him.

The sirens are getting closer and Dallas turns away from me to look out the front door once more.

"Get your head out of your ass for two seconds here and think about what you're saying," Dallas says angrily, his hands still wrapped tightly around my arms. "You were here questioning someone for a murder investigation. A murder investigation that you aren't supposed to be anywhere near."

His words flip a switch in my brain and all the fight leaves my body. He's right. What would I even tell the police when they got here? That I just happened to stop by the house of a man who worked with Richard Covington and it was just a coincidence that he was shot down right in front of me?

"You need to get the hell out of here right now."

I stare at Dallas, more confused than I've ever been. Why is he helping me? He should be making sure I get thrown in jail for what I've been doing.

"Why are you doing this?" I whisper.

"We don't have time for this. Get in your car and go. Now."

He pulls me against him and walks me through the doorway. He's made sure to position himself in such a way that I don't have to see Andrew lying on the ground behind him.

When I'm on the front porch, he finally lets go of me and I walk in a trance down the stairs and toward my car. The sirens are only a few blocks away now and I know I need to hurry. I run the rest of the way, fumbling my keys out of my coat pocket and wincing at the pain in my hands. I get in the car, start it up, and speed away from Andrew Jameson's house and Dallas, watching in my rearview mirror as blue-and-red flashing lights pull up to the curb where I was just parked.

A few hours later I hear my doorbell ring and I realize I've been sitting on my couch staring at nothing since I got home. I should have showered. Or at the very least, washed the blood off my hands. At least I put on a fresh shirt.

Pushing myself up, I walk over to the door and look through the peephole. I'm not surprised to see Dallas standing on my front porch with his hands in his pockets.

I open the door and he walks right in without an invitation. I close the door and turn to see him pacing back and forth in the living room.

"What the hell were you thinking?" he finally says, coming to a stop with his hands on his hips.

Here we go again. He's going to tell me what an idiot I am and how I'm not cut out for this line of work. He's in *my* house and I'll be damned if I'm going to let him make me feel like crap.

Mirroring his pose with my hands on my hips, I let it fly. "I am sick and tired of people underestimating me. I might not have a lot of experience yet, but I'm good at what I do. I can solve this murder case!"

My chest is heaving and even though it feels good to let all of that out and not have it burning a hole in my chest, I have no idea what made me spew all of my insecurities at Dallas. I don't know why I care what he thinks of me.

"Lorelei. Come on, snap out of it, baby. Look at me."

His words from earlier echo through my mind. He was so careful with me, almost sweet. It's like my subconscious knows there's a nice guy in there underneath all of that cockiness. A guy who was worried about me and made sure I didn't get in trouble.

He still hasn't said a word since my outburst and it's starting to make me uncomfortable.

"What, nothing to say now? No more insults or tips about how I'm just going to screw everything up?" I ask sarcastically, trying not to feel like a bug under a microscope as he stares at me. I'm sure he's just taking his time trying to think of some way to put me down.

Without saying a word, he takes a few steps in my direction and stops in front of me. I flinch when he wraps his hand around one of my wrists and flips it over, brushing his fingers over my palm.

"You didn't get all of the glass out," he tells me gruffly.

I pretend like his close proximity has no effect on me and stare at the top of his head as he brushes a tiny shard of glass out of a cut in my hand.

"What happened with the police?" I ask him.

Dallas drops my hand and picks up the other one, concentrating on searching every inch of it for stray glass. "I told them I was there following up a lead and we were ambushed. I said it all happened so fast that I didn't have time to pull my weapon."

I want to thank him for getting me out of there and not saying anything to the police, but I still have no idea why he's doing this. What's in it for him?

"Do you think they believed you?"

He lets go of my hand when he's satisfied that there's no more glass and looks up at me. I wrap my arms around myself, suddenly cold now that he's no longer touching me.

"Of course they bought it. They dusted for fingerprints while I was there. Please tell me you didn't touch anything when you went into the house. Doorframe, doorknob, anything like that?"

I shake my head no. The only things my hands touched were the floor and the side of Andrew's neck. Hopefully they didn't dust his body.

"Then we should be fine. They won't find your fingerprints and the people in that neighborhood hate cops. When they go door to door questioning neighbors, no one will tell them if they saw anything."

Dallas moves around me and walks to the door.

"Why are you doing this? Why did you help me?"

He pauses with the door open but doesn't turn around. "Maybe I just like the idea of you owing me one, Lawyer. I'm sure it will come in handy."

He's lying. His words don't have their usual snarky tone and he won't meet my eyes.

"Just do me a favor. Start brushing up on your PI skills. I don't want to have to save your ass again anytime soon."

CHAPTER 8

N o. Absolutely not."
I pack my files into my rolling bag, pull up the handle, and head toward the door of Fool Me Once.

Kennedy grabs my arm and spins me around. "Lorelei, come on. I know the guy gets on your nerves, but he needs help. And hey, maybe if you do this for him, he'll stop being such an ass."

I really cannot believe I'm contemplating this right now. After Dallas left my house the other night, I thought maybe things were going to change between us. I wasn't expecting friendship or anything crazy like that, but at least civility. I called Stephanie Covington the following day to question her some more about Andrew Jameson and within a half hour of ending the call, I received a text from Dallas that read, *"Stop talking to my suspects. Didn't you learn your lesson by almost getting shot?"*

So much for being civil.

"Dallas Osborne is never going to stop being an ass," I tell her, glancing at my watch.

"This is true. But at least he's pretty to look at," she jokes.

I glare at her.

"Come on, Lorelei. Regardless of what a jerk he is, he still helps us out here big time. We owe him for helping Paige bring down Vinnie DeMarco last month."

It frustrates me that she's right. Dallas has dropped what he's doing several times to help Kennedy with past cases, and he was a big help when Paige got herself into a bind with one of the biggest crime families in the state. But that doesn't mean I have to drop what *I'm* doing because he suddenly needs a lawyer to rescue him.

"Tell me again what the charges are."

Kennedy fist pumps and I groan. "This does not mean that I'm saying yes."

"Whatever. You're totally going to do it. The dumbass never paid a speeding ticket so they put a warrant out for his arrest. He pissed off the officer who issued the ticket and the guy got a rush put through on the warrant without Ted knowing about it first. God only knows what he said to the guy. Luckily, Ted was able to sweet-talk this idiot into not throwing Dallas in jail. But he's still being charged with a misdemeanor for failure to pay. If he's charged, he's going to lose his license."

I can't help but laugh. "You have got to be kidding me."

"I can tell by the gleam in your eye that you can't wait to do this."

Oh, I definitely can't wait to do this.

⸻

Walking down the aisle of one of the smaller courtrooms, I see Dallas sitting at the front table by himself, nervously tapping his fingers on the wood. The judge enters the room from his chambers and sits down at his bench just as I slide into the chair next to Dallas. He looks over at me in surprise.

"What the fuck are—"

I cut him off. "Keep your mouth shut, your head down, and don't say one word unless I tell you to."

"All rise!"

I immediately stand and Dallas scrambles to get up, still in shock, I'm sure, from my showing up.

"The Honorable Judge Anderson, presiding."

Dallas leans over and puts his mouth close to my ear, whispering in irritation, "When I told Ted I needed a lawyer, I meant someone good."

For once, I don't let his words bother me. He's in hot water and he needs me. And believe me, I already decided on the way over here how he's going to pay.

"Be seated," Judge Anderson announces. "Case number 479862, the State versus Dallas Osborne. Are all parties present?"

"Yes, Your Honor," I answer.

While the judge makes a few notes on the court documents in front of him, I open up the file I got from Judge Anderson's paralegal on the way in.

"Seriously? Seventy-five in a twenty-five?" I scold Dallas in a whisper as I look over the ticket he got eight months ago.

"Some of us have important jobs where we need to rush to catch bad people," he whispers back sarcastically.

It takes everything in me not to stand up, waltz right out of the courtroom, and let them throw him in jail.

"Counselor, how does your client plead?" Judge Anderson asks.

Dallas starts to speak and I reach over and clutch his arm to get him to shut up.

I stand. "Not guilty, Your Honor."

Judge Anderson looks out over the top of his glasses at me. "Counselor, you do realize your client was going fifty miles an hour over the speed limit and never appeared in court to pay his fine, correct?"

"I should have just locked myself up," Dallas mutters to himself.

Kicking his ankle under the table, I address the judge. "Yes, Your Honor. I'm perfectly aware of the charges being brought against my client. What the court fails to understand though is that my client works closely with the South Bend police force to help them solve cases. He also owns an extremely busy private investigation firm on the side. One, if not both, of these jobs requires him to rush to crime scenes to get crucial evidence to put murderers, kidnappers, and other extremely harmful individuals in this county behind bars. If I'm not mistaken, Your Honor, you yourself have recommended Osborne Investigations to several of your coworkers and other government employees because you were aware my client would do whatever it took to find justice. I realize, though, this doesn't excuse his failure to pay the fines, Your Honor. My client takes these charges very seriously and would be happy to pay those fines today to avoid jail time."

Judge Anderson taps his pen against the legal pad in front of him for several long minutes before he finally speaks. "Counselor, please approach the bench."

"Son of a bitch. Thanks for nothing," Dallas whispers angrily.

I ignore him, walking out from behind the table and up to the front of the courtroom. Judge Anderson and I debate for several minutes and finally come to a conclusion. He writes a few notes down on the papers in front of him, signs them, and hands them off to the paralegal sitting next to him.

I make my way back to the table and flip my legal pad closed, paying no attention to the imploring look Dallas is giving me that I see out of the corner of my eye.

"Mr. Osborne, please stand. In the case of the State versus Dallas Osborne, you have been found not guilty. You can pay your fines with the cashier on the way out. Case dismissed."

Sliding my legal pad and pen into my bag, I turn and begin walking down the aisle of the courtroom.

"Lorelei, wait!"

I wipe the smile off of my face and turn to Dallas.

He stands there looking at me for several long minutes as defendants for the next case start filing in around us.

Really, is it that hard for him to say thank you?

"I just . . . um, well . . ."

Rolling my eyes at him, I start to turn around and walk away again, but he stops me with a hand on my arm.

"Look, I just . . . what's with the outfit?"

He nods at my black Armani pencil skirt and white button-down.

"Seriously? I just prevented you from spending time in jail and you're asking me about my clothing?"

He runs his hand through his hair and shrugs. "I thought maybe with that sexy getup the other night you were turning over a new leaf. Trying to break out of the boring lawyer mold."

I swear to God this man's mood swings are going to be the death of me.

"This boring lawyer just saved your rear end," I remind him.

He laughs and shakes his head at me. "You know, you can actually say the word 'ass' out loud. You had no problem telling me—what was it again? That I'd be sitting there with my dick in my hand?"

My cheeks flush in embarrassment. I still can't believe I actually said that to him.

"So what did you say to the officer who gave you the ticket that made him so angry?" I ask, moving the talk away from his nether regions.

Dallas laughs and the corner of his mouth curves up, showcasing a dimple. "He was taking his sweet-ass time walking back and forth between his car and mine while he checked my background. I may or may not have told him that if he laid off the doughnuts he'd be able to move faster."

I shake my head at him in disapproval.

"Hey, you can't fault me for being honest," he says.

"Well, as thrilling as this was, I have a meeting in five minutes. Oh, and don't worry about thanking me or paying me for the time I just wasted bailing you out. I've already decided how you'll pay me back."

This time, I turn and walk away quickly before he can stop me.

"What's that supposed to mean?" he yells to my back.

Without turning around, I raise my hand in the air and give him a finger wave.

"We'll be in touch soon, Mr. Osborne."

As I push through the courtroom doors, I hear Dallas shout my name, but I ignore him and continue walking.

I made a deal with the judge that Dallas would do twenty hours of community service by giving talks to a few of the local high schools on the dangers of speeding. I think for now, I'll keep that little tidbit to myself. First, I plan on making Dallas pay me back by forcing him to work with me on this murder investigation . . .

CHAPTER 9

"Hello, darling! How's work?"

I sigh into the phone. "Doug, please stop calling me 'darling.' It's uncomfortable."

My ex-husband huffs and I can tell he's pouting. "Oh, Lorelei, don't be like that. I was just calling to see if you'll be bringing a date to the wedding in a few weeks. You're coming, right? We never got your response card."

If you ask Doug, he'll tell you our divorce was one hundred percent amicable. He assumes we should still be best friends even though he failed to mention he was gay. When he MARRIED ME. I tried to remain mad at him, but it's difficult. He really does make a wonderful friend.

"And just so you know, it's perfectly okay if you're coming alone. Gary has a single cousin who is just dying to meet you," Doug adds.

Perfect. My gay ex-husband is trying to set me up. Is there anything more humiliating?

"Of course I'll be at the wedding, but if you put me at a table with anyone's single cousin, I will wear white and ruin your entire color scheme," I tell him.

"Well, now you're just being cruel. I'll put you down for a plus one just in case. We'll talk soon. Kisses!"

I end the call and throw my cell phone down on my desk a little too forcefully.

"You know, in this instance, it's okay to call him an asshole," Kennedy tells me as she walks over and drops a file on my desk.

"I can't call Doug that. He means well, I guess."

Paige walks through the door with a tray of coffees in her hand. "Who means well?"

Kennedy pulls a cup off of her tray. "Doug. He just called to talk about the wedding."

Paige rolls her eyes and sets the tray down on my desk. "Screw him. He's an asshole."

"See? I told you." Kennedy smiles. "Come on, say it. 'Doug is an asshole.'"

Grabbing my own cup of coffee, I open the lid and blow on it. "Doug is not an . . . *asshole.* He's happy. He's getting married. I can't be angry at him for that."

"The fuck you can't!" Kennedy argues. "He married you when he knew all along he was gay. Asshole. You caught him screwing a man in your living room. Asshole. He still invited you to his wedding. HUGE asshole."

I take a sip of my coffee. "Can we talk about something else, please? I don't want to think about this wedding until absolutely necessary."

Kennedy perches her hip on the edge of my desk. "Fine. Let's talk about your vocabulary. Say 'fuck.'"

I stare at her in irritation.

"Come on, I know straight-laced Lorelei is just dying to break out of her shell and scream some obscenities. How are you going to work side by side with Dallas Osborne and not call him a fuckhead at least once?" Kennedy asks.

I told the girls all about the plan I hatched in court the other day.

They thought it was brilliant, but Kennedy has been trying to prepare me the last few days by turning me into a gutter mouth.

"If I think a situation warrants it, I will swear. I don't need to practice," I tell her.

Kennedy shrugs. "Hey, I'm just looking out for you. I don't want you to lose your shit one of these days and yell something embarrassing like, 'You're a shitdamn hell fuck!'"

Ignoring her, I look at Paige. "Did you send that e-mail to Dallas?"

She smiles and takes a seat at her desk across from me. "Oh, I sure did. And I blacked out half of the information like you suggested and told him if he wanted the rest of it, he'd need to contact you."

I asked Paige to scan the e-mails we found in Richard Covington's home and send them to Dallas. Minus a few pertinent details like who they were from and when they were sent.

"I also blacked out every fourth word just to mess with him," Paige says with a laugh.

"He's going to be pissed," Kennedy says with a smile.

My cell phone starts to ring and, looking at the display, I see that it's Dallas.

"Well, speak of the devil. That was fast."

Clearing my throat, I answer the phone in my best professional voice. "Lorelei Warner, how may I help you?"

"Where's the rest of the information in these e-mails?" Dallas asks without preamble.

"Good morning to you too, Mr. Osborne. What e-mails are you referring to?" I ask pleasantly.

Paige and Kennedy cover their mouths to contain their laughter.

"Cut the crap. I get it. This is my punishment for your getting me out of that ticket. Fine. I'll leave you alone so you can play detective. I won't say another word about your lack of skills. Just give me the rest of the information in those e-mails."

I pick up a pen and tap it against my desk. While the idea of his leaving me alone actually has some merit, that's not what this is all about. I want him to eat his words. I *can* do this job.

"You avoided thirty days in jail and didn't lose your license because of me," I remind him.

"Yeah, well, I still had to pay a two-thousand-dollar fine," he complains.

I grind my teeth. "It was supposed to be four thousand dollars. I'm going to need a little more than just your turning the other cheek while I 'play detective.'"

I hear him growl into the phone. "Fine. What do you want?"

Kennedy starts waving her hands in the air frantically.

"Could you hold, please?" I press my palm against the mouthpiece and hold the phone away from me.

"What?" I hiss at her.

"Tell him he's an asshole and you deserve some fucking respect!" Kennedy shouts.

Shaking my head at her, I pull my hand away from the mouthpiece and press the phone back against my ear.

"Sorry about that. Where was I? Oh, yes. Well, I've decided that you and I will start working together to solve this case and when I find out who did it, you can just give me your fee from the police department," I inform him.

He barks out a laugh. "When hell freezes over."

I smile to myself. "Bundle up. We'll get together this weekend to go over the rest of the information in those e-mails. Have a nice day!"

Ending the call without letting him say another word, I sit there for a few minutes and stare at my phone.

"I still think you should have called him an asshole, but you did good," Kennedy tells me.

"So, when are you going to meet up with him? Do I get to dress you again?" Paige asks excitedly.

"I have dinner at my parents' house on Friday night, so it will have to be after that," I remind them.

Everyone is silent for a few minutes. They know this is the weekend I planned on telling them about my job here and how I wasn't sure if being a lawyer was what I wanted to do for the rest of my life.

"Well, then, I think you should definitely let Paige dress you," Kennedy informs me.

Paige jumps up from her chair and practically bounces over to us. "We can find something totally hot and badass for Lorelei and we can get your outfits for your romantic engagement weekend with Griffin while we're at it!"

Kennedy groans. "Do I really still have to buy new clothes for this?"

I gather my things. "Remember how you said you'd owe me one for being Dallas's lawyer? You'll go shopping with Paige and me and not say one single word. We get to dress you any way we see fit and you can't complain."

"Ooooh, you'll be like our own personal Barbie," Paige tells her with a laugh.

"You did NOT just say that to me."

As we walk out of the office, I ignore Paige and Kennedy as they bicker back and forth. A few hours of shopping might be just what I need to get my mind off of the coming weekend. I'm going to drop a huge bomb on my parents and then try to work with Dallas. Both events could be equally explosive.

CHAPTER 10

❧

My parents live in Hamilton County. It's about an hour-and-a-half drive from my home so I have plenty of time to think about what I'm going to say to them. And plenty of time to rethink the outfit Paige made me buy on our shopping trip.

As I pull up the drive to their palatial brick home, I take a deep breath before getting out of my car. I seriously consider getting back inside and driving to the nearest Neiman Marcus to buy a suit. It's not that I'm dressed unpleasantly; it's just that I'm not dressed for dinner with my parents. My mother will undoubtedly have on a dress and pearls and my father will be wearing one of his usual black suits.

Staring down at myself, I know that what I'm wearing is perfectly fine: a pair of black leggings with brown, knee-high slouch boots, a tan-and-black-striped long-sleeved shirt, and a black infinity scarf. As soon as Paige picked out this outfit I knew I had to have it. It may seem like everyday wear for some, but it's not something I have ever worn and I love it. My parents will definitely hate it.

Closing my eyes for a moment, I think about all of the reasons I want to be a private investigator. I think about how happy it makes me and how overjoyed I am that for the first time in my life, I look forward to waking up in the morning, knowing I'm going to do something exciting. I play these points on a continuous loop in my head as I walk toward the front door.

The rumbling of a car engine in the drive gives me pause. I turn to see a familiar black Mustang pull up behind my car and dread pools in my stomach.

I watch in horror as Dallas gets out of the car and saunters over to me. Even in my moment of despair I don't miss the way he takes me in from head to toe. I have an unnatural urge to touch my wavy hair, which Paige carefully sprayed into place, to make sure it still looks good.

"Well, don't you clean up nice," he says with a lopsided smile.

"What are you doing here?" I respond, whipping my head around to the front door to make sure my parents aren't standing there. If I'm lucky, they didn't hear the reverberation of his muffler coming up the drive and have no idea I'm here yet.

"I'm sorry; I thought you said we would be working together now," he tells me casually as he slides his hands into the front pockets of his jeans. "I swung by your place so we could have ourselves a little meeting, and when I saw you pulling out, I figured I'd follow you. I'm guessing you just failed to mention to me that you'd be meeting with Miles Harper tonight."

Oh, my God, this is not happening right now. Of all the times for him to be pompous and cocky . . .

"I can see by the shocked expression on your face that you didn't think I'd find out about Miles. Nice work blacking out his name on the e-mails, by the way, but I was able to figure out that information all on my own."

Maybe if I jump in my car right now, I can just tell my parents I had a flat tire and won't be able to make it to dinner.

"I didn't feel like wasting my time looking up his address. Figured you could handle that for me and I could just follow you." Dallas whistles appreciatively as he looks at the front of my parents' home. "No wonder you're a lawyer. Must be a pretty nice paycheck."

Perfect. And now he thinks the only reason I'm a lawyer is because it pays well. Won't he be surprised when he finds out I was bred for this job and further manipulated into it with years of guilt?

Wait, what am I saying? He's not going to find that out because he needs to leave right now. I need to get him away from here before they see him.

"This isn't Miles Harper's home; it's where my parents live! I'm here for dinner with them, not going behind your back to meet with Miles," I tell him, throwing my arms up in irritation.

I leave out the part about how I was fully planning on finding Miles after dinner. I'm too livid at his audacity right now to deal with semantics.

"Lorelei, what on earth are you doing standing out in the driveway? Mrs. Cooper has already set out the first course."

I freeze at the sound of my mother's voice.

"I wish you would have told me you were bringing a guest," she complains.

I watch her turn in the entryway, rushing back into the house, and know she's left to complain to my father about having to set an extra place, even if she hasn't set a table herself my entire life.

"Well, honey, what's for dinner?" Dallas says with a smile as he brushes past me and heads into the house.

— ·—

"So, Mr. Osborne, how did you meet Lorelei?"

I pause with my fork halfway to my mouth and try not to let the apprehension I'm feeling show. This is not how I wanted this evening to go. I was supposed to have a nice, quiet evening with my parents and then sit them down after dinner and calmly tell them my dreams for the future have changed.

Now, I'm stuck sitting across the table from Dallas.

"Well, sir, we work—"

My fork clatters onto the plate and I quickly interrupt him. "Actually, Dad, it's nothing too exciting. We met at the courthouse."

Dallas looks at me questioningly and I try to tell him with my eyes to please keep quiet and not ruin things for me.

"Lorelei, elbows off the table, please," my father reprimands.

I do as he asks and squeeze my hands together in my lap.

"So, you're an attorney then?" my father continues.

I watch as he stares at the tattoos on Dallas's arms peeking out from the edge of his T-shirt. It's obvious my father is judging him and it raises my hackles.

"Uh, no. I'm not an attorney. I own my own private investigation firm, and lately I've been working as a part-time detective with the South Bend police department," Dallas informs him.

He pushes his sleeves up higher on his arms and then crosses his arms in front of him. It's almost like he's daring my father to ask him about the tattoos.

"Lorelei, your hair is atrocious. Are you going through some sort of phase?" my mother asks, just to switch things up.

I grind my teeth together and pick up my fork. "No, I just thought I'd try something new."

Five minutes in this home and I already feel my determination fading.

My father digs the knife in a little deeper. "I played golf with Steve Burdick the other day. He said you've postponed a meeting with him three times in the last two weeks. That's not very professional, Lorelei. How do you expect to make partner with behavior like that?"

Steve Burdick is a partner at my firm and I know exactly why he wants to meet with me. I know he's going to offer me the partner position, and right now, I just don't know if I'm strong enough to turn it down. I keep hoping the longer I put it off, the more confidence I'll gain being a private investigator and it will make the decision easy.

"I'm sorry. I've just been very busy. I'll call him first thing Monday morning," I tell my father.

My eyes meet Dallas's across the table. He's uncrossed his arms and now has his fists resting on the table, clenching and unclenching them like he's mad about something. He stares at me with his brow furrowed.

I pull my gaze away when my father speaks again. "Yes, make sure you do that. It's uncomfortable for me when I run into colleagues and have to make excuses for you."

I can feel my face heating up with embarrassment. It's bad enough that I have to suffer through these types of conversations every time I'm with my parents, but it's a million times worse now that Dallas is here witnessing my humiliation.

"Mr. Warner, I'm sure you're already aware of this, but your daughter is amazing at her job. I've seen her in action," Dallas informs him.

My father wipes the corner of his mouth with his napkin and sets it on the table. I watch in fascination as Dallas goes about eating, not even realizing that my father is glaring at him.

"Yes, well, we've made sure she's kept on the right track. As long as she doesn't make any more foolish mistakes her future will be set."

Dallas snorts and shakes his head.

"I'm sorry; is there something you'd like to say?" my father asks him.

Any other man would cave before my father, but not Dallas. If anything, he sits up taller and makes sure to smirk at my mother as he places both of his elbows on the table.

"Oh, there are a lot of things I'd like to say, but they probably aren't appropriate for dinner conversation. Your daughter doesn't make foolish mistakes. If anything, she's too perfect. She's smart and she's a hard worker. As her parent, that should be something to be proud of."

I can't hide the shock from my face at the words that leave Dallas's mouth. Is he actually sticking up for me? And why does this make me so happy and angry all at the same time? I should be sticking up for myself. But just like any other time I'm around my parents, I feel like nothing I say matters.

"Of course we're proud of her. We just want to make sure she's making smart choices in her life. The way she's dressing and her careless attitude at work worries us that she's being influenced," my father replies, looking pointedly at Dallas and his tattoos.

Dallas stares him down and my father actually has the intelligence to look away. Unfortunately, my mother decides it's time to rejoin the conversation.

"Have you spoken to Doug lately? How is he?"

I shouldn't be shocked that she's bringing Doug up. She does it every time we speak. But doing it in front of Dallas is a new low even for her. It's not every day I bring a man to dinner. Obviously they must suspect we're dating, even if it's the furthest thing from the truth. In her mind, there's nothing wrong with speaking of her daughter's ex right in front of another man. And now Dallas gets to add one more thing to his long list of inadequacies about me.

"He's fine, Mother. How are the plans coming along for the Make-A-Wish event next month?" I ask, hoping that she'll get the hint and change the subject.

She doesn't. "I just don't understand why the two of you couldn't work things out. You were so happy and you had a wonderful life together. Your father and I have had our differences, but we've always managed to work them out."

She looks at me. Like it's my fault because I didn't try hard enough. I've heard this same speech so many times I could recite it by heart.

"How exactly would you suggest I work out the tiny little problem of him being gay? Marriage counseling? An intervention?"

Dallas snorts and at first, I assume he's laughing at me. When I look over at him, though, he's giving me a look of encouragement.

"There's no need for sarcasm, Lorelei," my father scolds. "You just didn't spend enough time taking care of him. A wife should always put her husband first."

Dallas can see the wounded look come across my face and once again, he tries to come to my rescue.

"If you ask me, this Doug person is the one who screwed up. Any man would be lucky to have Lorelei as his wife."

I swallow the lump in my throat as I stare at him across the table. He winks at me and smiles.

My father, of course, can't leave it alone. He has to add his two cents. "Well, we didn't ask you, young man. Someone such as *you* wouldn't understand the importance of a person's standing in the community. Lorelei has a reputation to uphold and we just want to be certain she remembers that. Doug was a good catch. He had a respectable job with the clerk of courts and would have never thought that coming to dinner in jeans and a T-shirt was appropriate."

I've officially had enough.

Throwing my napkin down on the table, I stand abruptly, my chair scraping across the hardwood floor of the dining room. It's one thing when they insult me, but I won't allow them to look down on Dallas. They don't even know him. It strikes me that I really don't know him either, but that's beside the point. He tried to stick up for me and now it's my turn.

"Lorelei, sit down. We aren't finished with dinner," my father says in exasperation.

"Well, *I'm* finished. I've lost my appetite."

I see Dallas staring at me. His eyes are soft and encouraging. I can practically feel his strength floating across the table and wrapping itself around me.

I glare at my father. "I'm not a good enough lawyer because I don't work as hard as you'd like and I wasn't a good wife because I worked too much. It's never enough for you. And believe me, it's impossible to forget all the responsibilities you've strapped me with. You remind me every single day that I'm not living up to your expectations. I come here tonight wearing something other than a perfectly pressed suit and you immediately assume I've gone to the dark side. You can berate me all you want, but don't you dare look down on him," I fire back, pointing at Dallas. "You think he's a negative influence? Why? Because he doesn't fit in your perfect mold and he has tattoos? Well guess what? I have a fucking tattoo and I HATE being a Goddamn lawyer."

My mother gasps, but I ignore her. I'm on a roll.

"I've missed all those meetings with Steve because I'm part owner of a private investigation company and I love it. I don't want to spend my days in three-piece suits, kissing everyone's ass just so I can get ahead. First thing Monday morning I'm walking into Steve's office and telling him he can shove his partnership right up his fucking ass."

And with that, I storm out, making sure to let the door slam behind me because I know my father hates it.

CHAPTER 11

P acing back and forth in the driveway, I can hardly believe what just happened. Did I really tell my father off? Too bad Kennedy wasn't here to see it. I feel like she would be extremely proud.

I hear the door open behind me and figure it's my mother coming outside to tell me how appalling my behavior was. When I see Dallas charging down the steps toward me, my heart starts thumping wildly in my chest. I'm sure he's coming out here to make fun of me and my terrible family.

"Look, I'm not really in the mood for you to—"

My words are cut off as he grabs my face with his hands and crushes his lips to mine. Dallas Osborne is a force of nature. He's hard around the edges, crass, and full of attitude. His kiss matches his personality: It's rough and all consuming.

It's the best thing I've ever felt.

His tongue immediately pushes past my lips and he backs me up against the hood of my car. I moan into his mouth and grab fistfuls of his hair in my hands, holding him close and letting him plunge his tongue deeper. He keeps one hand on my face and slides the other down the side of my body, cupping my ass in his hand and pulling me against him.

I've been kissed by plenty of men in my life. They were all the same or variations of the same—polite, soft kisses that left me wanting more. Dallas doesn't kiss me like I'm a piece of crystal. He kisses me like he wants to break me and doesn't care if he leaves a few scars behind. My lips already feel bruised from the attack of his mouth and it's the most delicious pain I've ever experienced.

His arm tightens around my waist and my toes leave the ground as he holds me against his body, his tongue pushing against my own. One of my legs slides up around his hip and I anchor him to me, pulling him in tighter so I can feel him against me. I slide my arms around his neck, pulling him closer. I can feel every inch of his hard body and it just makes me want more. I've never felt fire like this or passion this explosive. It doesn't even matter that we're standing in my parents' driveway, leaning against the hood of my car. I want his naked body against mine and to feel him moving inside me.

He suddenly breaks the kiss and pulls his mouth away from mine. My heart is pounding. At least I'm not alone. With our chests pressed tightly together, I can feel his own heart thudding against mine.

When I can finally breathe again, I speak. "What the hell was that?"

Dallas tightens his hold on me. "Do you really have a tattoo?"

I'm sorry, what? He storms out here and kisses me like that and the first question he asks is about my tattoo?

"Are you kidding me?" I fire back.

"Kind of. Not really. But to answer your question, I don't know what the hell that was, but I wish it would have happened sooner," he admits.

"You can't stand me. You put me down every chance you get. And you expect me to believe you wished you kissed me sooner?"

I feel like I just entered the Twilight Zone.

He just shrugs. "What can I say? You drive me crazy and for some strange reason, it's the biggest fucking turn-on. I've wanted to kiss you ever since you first called me a pompous ass."

Now this is a shocking development. I guess what they say about little boys picking on the girls they like on the playground when they're younger is also true for adults.

"And for the record, watching you stand up to those assholes was the hottest thing I've ever seen. That, and hearing you say the word 'fuck,'" he adds with a smile.

I look away from him in embarrassment. "I think I took that a little too far. They're probably never going to speak to me again."

He shrugs. "Fuck it. They're not worth it. If they can't see how amazing you are, they don't deserve to have you in their life."

All of this insight coming from him is a little shocking. I mean, I thought he felt the exact same way about me as they did.

I push away from him and slide away from my car. I need some distance. This is a little too much right now. I just spilled my guts to my parents and now Dallas is telling me he thinks I'm amazing. I don't know what to think.

"You'll have to forgive me if I don't exactly believe what you're saying right now. You've taken every opportunity to tell me I don't know what the hell I'm doing. You put me down left and right and I'm always second-guessing myself, wondering if I really am making a mistake."

He grabs my arms and pulls me back to him, bending down to look into my eyes. "Let's get one thing straight here. I admit I'm an asshole most of the time. But I have never underestimated you. I've been waiting for months to see that spitfire come out of you that I knew was hiding in there somewhere."

"Right. So your telling me outside of Stephanie Covington's house last week that I'm in over my head and I should go back to the courtroom was what? Tough love?"

The words tumble from my mouth and I immediately want to take them back. Do I really want him to know I've been dwelling on what he said to me every single day since then?

He sighs and pulls me against him. The warmth of his body feels so good that I instantly slide my arms around his waist even though I'm confused by what is happening.

"Why do you have to question everything? You told your parents where to stick it and now we don't hate each other. Much. We should be celebrating this momentous occasion, preferably by getting naked," Dallas informs me with a grin as his arms tighten around me.

"As much as I'm enjoying standing out here not hating you, I think we should probably leave. My parents will lose their minds if they see us out here like this. I think I've done enough damage for one night."

Dallas sighs. "You're probably right. Tearing your clothes off and fucking you on the hood of your car would probably push them over the edge."

And just like that, I'm hot all over again. I never thought hearing someone speak like this to me would be a turn-on. Out of anyone else's mouth, those words would have me smacking them across the face. But hearing them from Dallas, I want nothing more than to take him up on his suggestion.

"Well, I lied earlier when I told you I wasn't planning on doing any more investigating without you. I have the file for Miles Harper in my car. I was planning on stopping at his office when I left here."

Since he's been so honest with me tonight, I feel it's only right to go with full disclosure at this point.

He chuckles and pulls away from me, grabbing my hand and lacing his fingers through mine. "Yeah, I already figured as much. That's why I trailed your ass here. Crashing dinner with your parents was just an added bonus."

We walk around the front of my car and he opens my door for me.

"So are we really doing this? Working together without killing each other?" I ask as I slide into the seat and Dallas leans his arm on top of my open door.

"I'm not about to let you out of my sight, so that's affirmative."

I bristle at his words and glare at him.

"Don't give me that look. I know you're perfectly capable of handling this. It's for my own peace of mind, all right? I don't want to walk in on another scene like the one at Jameson's house."

His words calm me somewhat and I'm shocked that I believe him. And to be honest, it will be nice to have someone with experience by my side.

And someone who kisses so well.

"I'll follow you to Harper's office. Are they expecting you?"

I start my car and nod. "Yes. I called his secretary. He's staying at the office late for a meeting so he agreed to speak with me."

Dallas leans into the car and presses his lips to mine. I immediately get wrapped up in the kiss as his tongue slowly swirls around my own. He pulls back much too soon, pressing a kiss to my cheek before backing out of my car. He closes my door for me and I watch in my rearview mirror as he walks back to his car.

I'm working with Dallas Osborne without the need for blackmail or coercion and he just kissed me again like it was the most natural thing in the world. This is about to get very interesting. Or very messy.

CHAPTER 12

W ell, if it isn't Lorelei Warner. When my secretary told me you requested a meeting I almost couldn't believe it."

On the way up to Miles's office, Dallas gave me a few pointers. Be nice, but not too nice, and don't let on that we've seen the e-mail correspondence between Richard and him. The way Kennedy, Paige, and I came across those wasn't exactly legal and if anyone knows the ins and outs of the law, it would be Miles Harper. He graduated at the top of our class at Harvard and I found out in my research that any day now he's going to be appointed as a judge in Indiana. Rumor also has it that he's being positioned for a seat on the Indiana Supreme Court and that's why he's on such a fast track in his career.

Obviously, someone of his caliber would have a lot to lose if word got out that he was blackmailing one of the richest men in the state. Or if he killed him.

"Miles, it's so good to see you again."

I plaster a smile on my face as he rounds his desk and takes both of my hands in his before leaning in to kiss my cheek. My parents adore Miles, of course, and the few times we've seen each other, I've tolerated him. He throws his social standing and wealth around every chance he gets and it's nauseating.

"I must say, Lorelei, I like the new look," he tells me, staring me up and down. When Dallas did it earlier in the evening, it shot a thrill through my body. When Miles does it, I want to go home and shower.

"Hi, I'm Dallas Osborne. I work with Lorelei."

Dallas shoves his arm between me and Miles and I silently thank him for the interruption. Miles drops my hands and shakes Dallas's outstretched one.

"I thought maybe my secretary had made a mistake. When she told me Lorelei Warner was requesting a meeting as a private investigator, I nearly died laughing. So it's true you've given up your legal career for something frivolous? What is it you do exactly? Take down hardened criminals?"

Miles laughs at me mockingly and it makes my blood boil.

"Actually, yes, that's exactly what she does. If you don't mind, we're investigating the death of Richard Covington. We know the two of you worked together, so we'd just like to ask you a few questions."

Miles perches casually on the edge of his desk.

"Really? So the rumors are true. Lorelei Warner has kissed her stellar legal career good-bye to follow a lifelong dream of . . . what? Pretending she's a hard-ass among the dregs of society?" Miles says with a laugh. "Your parents must be having a field day."

Telling my parents off gave me such a high of satisfaction that I'm still floating on that. I would have no problem punching Miles in his smug face.

"Speaking of parents, how is your father doing? Is he going to be up for parole anytime soon?"

I know I shouldn't stoop to his level, but I can't help myself. Three years ago Miles's father, then president of Indiana State Bank, was convicted of embezzlement. Miles has had a hard time clearing the family name and working his way back up the social ladder. I know my point hits home when I see the smile vanish from his face.

In its place is barely concealed fury. Good. That's exactly what I want. A man fueled by anger is more likely to slip up.

"Ask your questions. I have work to do," Miles informs me through clenched teeth.

"How many years did you work with Richard Covington?" Dallas asks.

Miles tears his angry gaze from mine and looks over at Dallas. "I was part of his legal team for fifteen years—attorney-client privilege," Miles tells him, folding his arms in front of him.

It seems as though Miles is forgetting our mutual industry.

"Obviously we're not asking you to divulge any of Mr. Covington's legal confidences. But as I'm sure *you* are aware, the death of a client negates any previous attorney-client privilege if such information is necessary in solving a crime."

Miles glances over at me and sighs. "What exactly would you like to know?"

"We're just wondering if Mr. Covington mentioned anything to you about enemies. Maybe someone in the business world who had a grudge against him, or possibly a blackmail scheme gone wrong."

Dallas coughs into his hand and I know that's his warning to stop. I know I shouldn't have brought up that exact suggestion, but I couldn't help it. I don't like the way Miles is sitting here acting like he's better than everyone. He's the type of person who naturally assumes he's smarter than the average person and can get away with anything he wants.

Miles narrows his eyes at me and I can see the wheels turning in his head. He's wondering what I know.

"Richard made a lot of enemies over the years, naturally. A man with that kind of wealth doesn't go through life without pissing a few people off," Miles explains.

"Is there anyone that stands out to you, someone who threatened him or maybe made him uncomfortable?" Dallas asks.

Miles laughs and shakes his head. "Everyone made Richard uncomfortable. Over the years, he became suspicious of a lot of people. Everyone was out to get his money, everyone was jealous of him, everyone wanted to do him harm. It was a never-ending cycle with Richard."

"Did you have any problems with him?" I question.

Miles glares at me again. "I worked for him for fifteen years. Of course we had our problems. But I'm a professional. I make sure to keep any personal feelings I have separate from business."

Right. Until you decide you aren't making enough money and try to blackmail your largest client.

"Yes, well, sometimes it's hard to separate the two. Especially if you feel like you're underappreciated. From what I hear, Mr. Covington was very stingy with his money. Did you ever feel like you weren't being compensated enough for your troubles?"

Miles stands up from his desk and advances on me. "What exactly are you trying to suggest, Lorelei?"

He's standing a few inches from me and I watch as his nostrils flare. Instead of arguing his innocence, he immediately took offense to my line of questioning.

"She's not suggesting anything. We're just trying to get to the bottom of things," Dallas says calmly.

Miles continues to stare at me and doesn't move away.

He's trying to intimidate me by standing so close, but it won't work. I'm not backing down. "It must be really hard to work for someone with that kind of money. Someone who throws it away on charities and a new wife when you've stuck by him and gotten him out of some pretty precarious situations for so many years. It's almost like a slap in the face. I'm sure you feel like you deserve more for all of your trouble."

Silence fills the room for a few minutes, and then Miles composes himself with a step back. "I think we're done here."

He walks around his desk and begins shuffling papers. "Lorelei, the South Bend police department must be thrilled that you're working with them to solve this case. I'll be sure to tell Chief Goodson what an asset you are to their team when I meet with him this weekend for drinks. And Mr. Osborne, how wonderful of you to agree to work together with Lorelei in solving this case. Your superiors really should be made aware of the good work you're doing."

Dallas wraps his hand around my arm and begins pulling me back out of the office as Miles sits down at his desk and picks up his phone.

"If you think of anything that might be pertinent to this case, please give me a call," Dallas tells him as we head out the door.

"I'll be sure to," Miles says with a sickeningly sweet smile as he begins dialing his phone.

Dallas and I get on the elevator and ride down to the first floor in silence. We walk quickly to our cars parked side by side in the parking garage.

"I'm sorry; I shouldn't have pushed him so far. I made a mistake and now he's going to talk to the chief and we're both going to be screwed," I complain.

Dallas takes the keys from my hand and presses the unlock button before opening my door for me. "You didn't screw anything up. He was egging you on and you retaliated. I would have done the same thing."

I shake my head. "No, you wouldn't. You would have never slipped up like that in the first place by bringing up those stupid e-mails. I let my emotions get the better of me."

"I was two seconds away from punching that cocky bastard in the face. Believe me when I tell you I would have done the same thing. He realizes we know something and we're suspicious of him. That's why he pulled out the police card. He assumes he scared us and we're going to walk away."

Leaning against the doorframe of my car, I stare up at him. "Is it wrong that I really hope he killed Richard and Andrew so he can spend life in prison?"

Dallas laughs. "I'm right there with you. There's just something about him that I don't like. He's too sure of himself. It's like he didn't even feel the need to justify that he didn't do it because anyone would be a fool to accuse him."

He rests his hands on the hood of the car, caging me in. "Can I just say, watching you hand him his ass on a plate was so fucking hot."

I stare up at him, my heart beating so fast I'm sure he can hear it. This morning I hated him and couldn't stop thinking about all the ways I wanted him dead. Now that I've kissed him, all I can think about are his lips.

He starts to lean toward me and I feel butterflies in my stomach, my excitement at getting to kiss him again at an all-time high.

The sound of a car door slamming from another part of the garage cuts through the silence. Dallas shakes his head and moves away from me, the moment gone. "I better go. It's getting late and I need to make some notes on Miles."

Trying to hide my disappointment, I quickly look away from him. "I have to go too. I have an early court case in the morning."

Why do things feel awkward now? Maybe we're better off hating each other.

"I'll swing by your office later in the afternoon and we can go over our notes," Dallas tells me as I toss my purse inside the car.

"Are you sure you still want to work with me? If Miles goes through with his threat, you could get fired."

Dallas shakes his head in disagreement. "He's not going to do anything. He's guilty of something and he knows it. Even if he didn't kill Richard, he still tried to blackmail him. We both know he'd be disbarred if that ever got out. I'll meet you tomorrow and we'll go over everything and see what we missed. You're not getting out of working with me that easily."

He closes my door once I'm inside and I watch him walk over to his own vehicle. I still don't trust that Miles won't go right to the police and tell them what Dallas and I are doing, but for now, I'm going to trust Dallas and just hope I didn't mess up both of our careers.

CHAPTER 13

⤳

True to his word, Dallas showed up at the office the following evening. I had almost given up hope after not hearing from him all day and was calling myself all kinds of a fool for borrowing another one of Paige's outfits. The short black-and-white plaid skirt and long-sleeved black sweater that hangs off of one shoulder reminds me a little bit of a Catholic-school uniform. According to Paige, that's the point. She seemed to think Dallas wouldn't be able to concentrate on anything but kissing me when he saw me wearing this. Obviously she was wrong. We've been sitting here for two hours poring over our notes and he's barely looked at me.

I really am an idiot. He's probably regretting everything that happened in my parents' driveway. He knows kissing me was a bad idea for so many reasons, not the least of which is that we have a murder to solve, which should take precedence right now.

Since when did I turn into this pathetic woman who dresses for a man and worries if he wants her?

Since I was kissed by a man like Dallas Osborne, obviously.

"So we know Miles has an alibi for the morning Richard was shot, but that doesn't necessarily mean he didn't have something to do with it," Dallas states from his chair on the other side of my desk, pulling me out of my thoughts.

I watch for a moment as he reads over my notes and adds them to his. I made a few calls earlier and had found out Miles was in court the morning Richard was killed.

Getting up from my seat, I bring both of my arms above my head and stretch, closing my eyes and groaning as I work out the kinks. We've been sitting in the exact same spots for so long that my entire body is stiff as a board.

"He could have hired someone to kill Richard. Can you look into his bank accounts and see if there were any big transactions around that time?"

Dallas doesn't answer me. I open my eyes, drop my arms back to my sides, and see that he's staring at my stomach, not blinking. Glancing down, I realize my sweater inched up while I was stretching. I quickly tug it back down and turn away.

"Do you want some coffee? I'm going to make some coffee," I ramble as I walk to the kitchen in the back of the office.

I glance over my shoulder as I pull the coffeepot from the machine and catch Dallas quickly looking away from my bare legs. He mumbles something to himself that I can't decipher and then rubs his palms down the front of his face a few times.

What the hell am I doing? Who cares if kissing him was the most exciting thing that's happened to me in thirty-plus years? What does it matter if he regrets it and wants to keep things all business now? I'm an adult, for God's sake. I don't need to rely on anyone to make me happy. My life is finally going the way I want it to. I don't need a complication like Dallas Osborne. We'll just chalk up yesterday's make-out session to a result of heightened emotions after that disastrous dinner with my parents.

With a firm resolve to pretend like nothing ever happened between us, I finish setting up the coffeemaker and walk back over to my desk while it brews. Not ready to sit down again in my uncomfortable chair, I grab a file from next to Dallas and go over to Kennedy's desk, hopping up on top of it and crossing my legs.

"What about the day Andrew Jameson was shot? Did we check and see if Stephanie and Miles had alibis for that day?" I ask, flipping open the file and reading through the notes.

"Son of a bitch, I can't do this," Dallas suddenly mutters.

I look up from the file in confusion to see him jump up from his chair and pace back and forth in front of me.

"If you're tired, we can stop and pick back up in the morning."

Dallas laughs mockingly and runs his hands through his hair. "That's not going to help. I changed my mind. Maybe it's not a good idea for us to work together."

I slam the file down on the desk. "Oh, you have got to be kidding me with this shit! I knew something was up with you tonight. Here I thought you just regretted kissing me yesterday. Nice to know you just don't think I'm worthy to work with you and your amazing crime-solving abilities."

He finally stops pacing and turns to glare at me. "Will you cut it out with that crap? I have no doubt that you could solve this case without help from me or anyone. I told you that already."

"Yes, and obviously I was an idiot for believing you since it's only been twenty-four hours and you're already going back on your word," I tell him angrily. "Get the hell out of my office and stop messing with my fucking head!"

Dallas throws his hands in the air, but doesn't make a move to leave.

"I thought I could do this, I really did. I thought I could forget about what happened and be a professional. This case is a big fucking deal and I don't want anything getting in the way of that!" he shouts.

So I was right. He does *regret kissing me. Fine, that's perfectly fine.*

"Great, we're in perfect fucking agreement then!" I yell back.

I open my mouth to fire some insults at him and before I can even utter one more word, he closes the distance between us. His hands grab my face and he pulls me against his mouth.

A surprised squeak bursts out of me, but Dallas slides his tongue past my lips and I forget to care that we were just yelling at each other. Like yesterday, the kiss is hard and powerful and it takes my breath away. My arms immediately wrap around his shoulders and I pull his body between my legs, wrapping them around his hips. As his tongue pushes and slides through my mouth, he leans his body against mine until I have no choice but to let go of him and rest my hands on the desk behind me.

His lips leave mine and I groan in protest as he stares at me.

"Just so you know, we are NOT in perfect fucking agreement. I didn't regret kissing you yesterday. I just thought we needed to be professionals and maybe have some distance while we're working this case," he explains.

One of his hands leaves the side of my face and moves to my thigh, still wrapped around his hip. He slides his palm up my leg until it disappears under my skirt and he's cupping my ass.

I glance down between us and then back up at him. "This doesn't look like distance to me."

His palm glides back up and over my thigh and the tips of his fingers brush against the lacy scrap of my underwear between my legs. Another groan leaves my mouth and my body jerks when he brings his fingers back, running them up and down over the lace.

"It's your fault. You and that mouth of yours. And I really, really like this skirt," he admits quietly.

He dips his head and his lips make a trail of kisses up the side of my neck while his fingers slide my underwear to the side. I throw my head back to give him better access to my neck while the pads of his fingers glide through my wetness. My thighs ache with how tightly they're clutching to his hips, but I don't care. I want him to keep doing what he's doing and never move from this spot.

As his mouth makes its way to mine and his fingers work me into a mindless frenzy, I can think of nothing but how good it feels to let go and just feel. His lips find mine and his tongue plunges into my mouth at the same time that his fingers push inside of me.

With one hand holding me up on top of the desk, I move the other hand to the back of his head and hold him in place. His mouth and his tongue move in sync with his fingers between my legs: push and pull, slide and swirl. My hips move against his hand and I forget how to breathe when I feel my orgasm creeping up on me. I'm a mindless ball of need and I have no idea what's coming out of my mouth as he pushes me closer and closer to the edge with his expert fingers. His thumb circles me and I hear nothing but gibberish escaping my lips as my release explodes out of me. I clutch Dallas's hair so tightly that I'm afraid I pull a few strands out.

"Fuck, fuck, fuck!" I shout as the best orgasm I've ever had washes over me.

Dallas chuckles and brings his lips back to mine. He kisses me softly as I slowly come down from my high and my legs fall limply down from around his waist.

He pulls his hand from between my legs and rests it on the desk. The kiss continues for several minutes until I finally pull away.

"All right, we can still work together. As long as this can continue happening," Dallas tells me.

I don't say anything to him as he leans in and kisses me again. He was probably right the first time when he said this was a bad idea, but right now, I don't care to argue with him.

CHAPTER 14

I can't breathe in this thing," I complain, tugging up the front of my dress.

Paige sighs and smacks my hands to stop the tugging. "Quit your bitching. You look hot. Breathing is a luxury."

Staring at myself in the mirror, I actually have to agree with Paige. The dress she picked out for me to wear to Doug's wedding is breathtaking. Literally. It's so tight that I have to take small, short breaths. The dress is strapless with a plunging sweetheart bustline. Another reason why I should avoid breathing—my boobs are practically falling out of this thing already. It's cream with a black lace overlay and it molds perfectly to my body. The skirt stops a few inches below my butt, so sitting down or attempting to cross my legs might pose a problem as well.

"Kennedy, what do you think?" I ask, turning around to face her. She's sprawled across my bed on her stomach with her arms hanging down over the edge.

"It's a dress."

Paige rolls her eyes and grabs a can of hair spray, adding a few spritzes to my hair. She kept it wavy but pulled it back in a low, loose bun. "Don't ask her what she thinks. She thinks wearing jeans and a T-shirt is perfectly fine for a proposal."

Kennedy pushes herself up to her knees. "It IS perfectly acceptable. If I wear something fancy, Griffin will know that I know that he's going to propose. He can't know that I know."

"I have no idea what you just said," Paige grumbles. "So, how do you think he'll do it? Maybe put the ring in your dessert? Spell out 'Will you marry me' in rose petals on the bed?"

Kennedy scrunches up her face and shakes her head. "Oh, hell no. He better not do any of those things if he knows what's good for him."

"Kennedy, this is your engagement to the man of your dreams. Your best friend. The man you should have married instead of that lying, cheating sack of shit you DID marry. It should be huge and romantic," Paige complains.

"No, it should be small and to the point. I want to be curled up on the couch watching a Notre Dame game and have him hand me a ring along with a plate of salsa and chips."

It's Paige's turn to make a face. "I just don't understand you sometimes." She sets the hair spray down and takes one last look at me. "Seriously, I am a genius. You really should have invited Dallas as your plus one."

Walking over to my closet, I slip into my four-inch black-lace peep-toe Christian Louboutins. "Inviting Dallas to my gay ex-husband's wedding is not at the top of my to-do list."

Paige flops down on the bed next to Kennedy. "How many times have you sucked face with him now?"

I laugh uncomfortably. "Um, I don't know. I stopped counting."

Seven. Seven times I've had the pleasure of kissing Dallas so far. Seven mind-blowing times and as hard as it is to believe, each time gets better and better. We've spent every single day of the last week together going over notes for the case. Well, not every second was spent going over notes. Some of that time was spent kissing, tasting, touching, and doing everything except having sex. And everything but discuss what's going on with us now—not how he'd wanted to kiss me since the first moment he saw me, not how he tried to pretend like that first kiss never happened, or how absolutely insane it is that one day we hated each other and the next we can't keep our hands off of each other.

"You are such a bad liar, Lorelei. Anyway, I bet he would have said yes if you asked him to go to Doug's wedding with you," Paige tells me." Especially after he gave you an orgasm on Kennedy's desk."

Kennedy pops up from the bed and stares at me in horror. "WHAT? I've touched that desk this week! Jesus Christ, I'm going to have to bleach my hands!"

I really need to stop confiding in Paige; she can't keep her mouth shut.

Ignoring Kennedy's outburst, I look at Paige. "I didn't want to put him in that position. It was bad enough he had to witness how horrible my parents are; I don't think he's ready for a gay wedding."

Paige sighs. "Tell me again about the first time he kissed you. It's like something right out of a movie."

"Wait, did I hear about that? I just know you two haven't been able to keep your hands off of each other every time I see you in the office and now thanks to you I'll have to burn my desk. Did you do something weird for the first kiss?" Kennedy asks.

"Oh, my God, Kennedy! He stalked toward her like a tiger going for his prey. Didn't say a word, just slammed her up against her car and laid one on her," Paige tells her excitedly.

"He didn't exactly slam me up against the car."

Paige raises her eyebrow at me.

"It was more of a push. A really, really hot push."

"Nice. I knew you two would finally get your heads out of your asses and hump like rabbits," Kennedy says with a smile.

"There is no humping going on!"

Kennedy stares at me in shock. "What do you mean there's no humping going on? I saw him grab your ass the other day. Why isn't there humping?"

I shrug and walk over to my vanity to add some nude lip gloss to my lips.

"It's not like I don't want it to happen, it's just . . . it hasn't. I don't know. We get to a certain point and he always backs off. With the way he teeter-totters back and forth, who knows, he's probably changing his mind about me again."

Kennedy snorts. "Bullshit. I've seen the way he looks at you. He would throw you down on the floor of the office, screw you ten ways to Sunday, and still want more."

"Maybe he's waiting for you to make the first move. I mean, he was the one who kissed you first," Paige adds.

Make the first move? I wouldn't even know where to begin with someone like Dallas. I'm not used to a man like him—someone who takes charge so fully.

"I think you need to get drunk. Liquid courage works wonders," Kennedy says with a nod.

"I don't get drunk. You know that."

"You also don't wear anything other than a suit, swear like a truck driver, kiss hot-as-balls men, or solve murders. I'm pretty sure you're already out of your comfort zone, Lorelei. Might as well add one more thing to the list," Paige says with a laugh.

She's right. And I've never been happier. I just don't know if I'm ready to throw that much caution to the wind right now.

"As much fun as it is to talk about humping and drinking, what's going on with the case?" Kennedy asks.

"It's such a mess. I still think his ex-wife is hiding something, but Dallas disagrees. She's never been in any kind of trouble, never done anything shady that would make anyone suspect her, but there's just something about her I don't trust."

Paige laughs and cocks her head at me. "Um, could it be the fact that you think Dallas slept with her?"

I huff indignantly. "No! It has nothing to do with that."
Much.

"Did you even ask him if he slept with her? That doesn't seem like something Dallas would do," Kennedy adds.

Of course I haven't asked him. That would just scream "jealousy." I'm not jealous of Stephanie Covington. Even though she's ten years younger than I am and has the body of a porn star.

"It doesn't matter. He doesn't think we need to question her again, so we aren't. We're doing everything together so I'm just going to go along with it."

"Just because you're playing nice doesn't mean you have to do everything he says. If you have a gut instinct about something, you should always go with it. Or at least argue your case. I've heard you know a thing or two about doing that," Kennedy says with sarcasm.

I shake my head at her. "Fine. I'll mention it to him again. He's just convinced that Miles is guilty. I'll admit, the guy is slime, but I just don't see him shooting someone in cold blood. He's kind of all talk. And he's got an alibi for the time frame that Richard was killed," I tell them.

"Well, don't back down. You've come a long way, Grasshopper, but there is still more to learn," Kennedy says in her best kung-fu voice.

Just then, Snowball jumps up onto the bed right next to her and hisses.

"Oh, my God, seriously? Get the fuck away from me, fur ball!" she shouts.

This just makes the poor cat angrier. She stands up on her hind legs and bats her paws angrily against Kennedy's arm.

"OW! You are such an asshole!"

Rushing over to the bed, I pick Snowball up and carry her to the door, tossing her out into the hallway, where she runs away hissing and growling.

"Seriously, what is that cat's problem?" Kennedy complains, examining the scratches on her arm.

"Cats can sense when people hate them," Paige tells her.

"Of course I fucking hate her! All she does is bitch at me. She's worse than my father," Kennedy argues.

"Okay, I think I'm ready to watch my ex-husband get married to the man of his dreams," I tell them, spinning around slowly with my arms out.

Kennedy whistles and Paige claps.

"If I was a lesbian, I would totally bang you. Just sayin'," Kennedy tells me.

"Have fun at the wedding, get drunk, and then give Dallas a booty call," Paige says with a laugh.

I shake my head at both of them, grab my black clutch off of my dresser, and head out. I'd much rather stay home and work on the case, but I need to get this over with. It's time to say good-bye to one chapter of my life.

CHAPTER 15

D arling, you look stunning," Doug tells me, holding my hands and kissing each cheek.

I smile at him and take in his black Armani suit. "And you look quite dashing yourself. I'm so happy for you, Doug."

I realize it's true as soon as the words leave my mouth. I thought I would be bitter and angry being here at his wedding, but I'm not. Aside from his being gay, it's glaringly obvious we weren't meant to be married. Neither one of us was truly happy when we were together. We kept who we were buried deep inside. Looking back now, walking in on him with another man and then ending our marriage was the right thing for both of us.

"I'm so glad you could be here today, Lorelei, especially after everything that happened between us. It means so much to me."

I can tell he's getting choked up. I don't want him to have any regrets. This is his day and he should be ecstatic. A waiter passes by with a tray full of champagne and I quickly grab two glasses, handing one to Doug.

"Now is not the time to be maudlin. Drink up and be happy."

We clink our glasses together. Doug takes a sip and I down my entire glass in three swallows. Setting my glass on the bar, I grab the arm of another waiter and snatch a second glass off of his tray.

Doug's jaw drops as I chug this one as well.

"Lorelei Warner, are you going to get drunk tonight?" he asks with a laugh.

I nod my head. "I was thinking about it. Gary's cousin hasn't left me alone the entire evening. I thought I told you not to seat him anywhere near me?"

Doug laughs and has the decency to look guilty. "Sorry, darling. Gary was sure you and Niles would hit it off."

"Five minutes after he met me, he asked if I wanted to go out to his car and smoke pot. Then he told me I reminded him of his mother and immediately asked if we could make out."

Niles is the reason why I've had three glasses of champagne so far. Wait, no, make that five.

Doug laughs again and pats me on the arm. "I'm sorry. If it makes you feel any better, Niles's mother is stunning."

"It does NOT make me feel any better, thank you very much. You're lucky this wedding is open bar," I scold.

"It's about time you let loose. How is that new case you're working on? I'm seething with jealousy that this is your life now. So exciting."

It makes me feel good to hear this from Doug. While it's true that my parents have always adored him and he played the part of son-in-law to a T, he's always had my back and been a good friend.

"It's hard work, but it's exhilarating. I don't know how close we are to figuring things out, but hopefully something will develop soon," I tell him.

"Gay men are never good at keeping secrets, so I'm sure Richard would have told someone *something* that will help you," Doug says, looking away from me to wave and smile at a guest.

"Wait, what? Richard was gay?"

Doug turns back to me. "Well, that's the rumor I heard from a few people. I myself always wondered about him. According to some people, he was the most homophobic man they've ever met. He doth protest too much . . ." Doug trails off.

"Since you seem to be in the know, did you ever hear anything about Miles Harper being gay? You remember him, right? He went to school with us and is practicing law at my father's old firm."

It's a long shot, but who knows? I'm willing to try anything at this point. Maybe that's the secret Miles was trying to blackmail Richard with—the fact that Richard was gay. Maybe the two of them were lovers. Could Miles have killed Richard in anger because Richard wouldn't give him more?

"Oh, I definitely remember him. If only it were true. That man is gorgeous. I haven't heard anything, but I could ask around for you," he tells me.

"I've never seen such magnificent flower arrangements. I always knew Doug could do anything."

I whip my head around at the sound of my mother's voice.

"Mother, what are you doing here?" I turn to Doug. "What is she doing here?"

Considering how adamant she was that the two of us should work things out and how she wouldn't hear a word of it whenever I tried to explain about Doug being gay, her being at this wedding right now is nothing short of astonishing.

"Doug invited me. I must say I wasn't sure what to expect. But I'm having a wonderful time."

"Where's Dad? Did he come with you?" I ask.

Not that I want to see him, but he might be able to shed some light on why in the world my mother would ever step foot in a gay wedding celebration.

"Your father is at home with . . . how do you say it? A stick up his ass. Actually, he's been sleeping in the guest house since your visit," she informs me.

I'm stunned into silence. I don't know if it's the champagne or not, but my head is spinning.

"Breathe, Lorelei," Doug tells me with a laugh. "Your mother called and told me the three of you had a very unpleasant dinner a week ago. I gave her some advice on how to handle things, but I didn't expect she'd go at it so wholeheartedly."

My mother smiles at me and grabs both of my hands. "Lorelei, I would just like to apologize for the way I've behaved. I realized after you left that you're doing something I've always wanted to do—be my own person. I'm envious of you. So I told your father where to stick it and kicked him out of the house."

"Oh, my God!" I exclaim in shock.

"Do you know I've never had an orgasm with your father? And I signed up for a pole-dancing class. You should go with me."

"Mom!" I scold in embarrassment, glancing around to make sure no one heard her.

Doug is too busy laughing to care.

It's impossible for me to even try to say anything more. Turning away from her in a daze, I signal to the bartender. "Bourbon, straight up. And keep them coming."

———

I giggle softly to myself when the cab driver asks me where I'm going. Where *am* I going? My face feels tingly. I tell him to hold on for a second and pull my phone out of my purse.

It takes me a few tries and a few more giggles to punch in the right number.

Paige answers on the first ring. "Did you have a good time?"

I snort in a very unladylike fashion and hiccup. "I had a FAB-ULOUS time! My mother's never had an orgasm!"

I laugh so hard that my stomach hurts.

"Oh, my God. You're drunk! Why am I missing this?" Paige asks.

"I feel funny. Everything is funny. I want to have sex with Dallas right now."

The cab driver stares at me through the rearview mirror and I wave to him.

"Get your ass to his house PRONTO! Now is your chance. Remember what Kennedy said: liquid courage."

Right. Liquid courage. I have that in spaces. Or spades. Whatever.

Blowing Paige a few kisses through the phone, I hang up and toss the phone in my clutch.

"Take me to Dallas's house!" I tell the driver excitedly.

He throws his arm over the back of the seat and turns around. "Where does Dallas live?"

I don't know. Where DOES Dallas live?

Pulling my purse onto my lap, I dig my phone out again and call him.

"What are you doing calling me? I thought you had a wedding to go to?" Dallas answers. I can hear his smile through the phone and it makes me feel all warm and fuzzy. Or maybe that's the bourbon talking.

"Where do you live?"

He laughs. "Um, on Highland Street, why?"

"Driver, take me to Highland Street!"

The cab driver shakes his head and pulls the car away from the curb.

"Lorelei, are you drunk dialing me?" Dallas asks in shock.

"I can neither confirm nor deny this statement, Your Honor," I tell him, dissolving into another fit of giggles. "My mother bought an orgasm. And my father's never given her a pole dance."

Dallas barks out a laugh. "Wow. That must have been some wedding. How long before you get here?"

"I don't know. But make sure you're not wearing any pants."

I end the call and let my head flop to the back of the seat.

I must have dozed off because a few seconds later, I hear Dallas's voice.

"It's okay; I've got her. Keep the change."

The back door opens and I sit up as Dallas leans into the car and pulls me out. I lose my footing on the curb when I step out and he wraps both of his arms around me and pulls me against him. He smells so good and he's so warm. I snuggle my face into his chest and take a deep breath.

He slams the door closed and the cab takes off. "Did you just sniff me?"

I look up at his face and see that he's smiling. "You smell yummy."

He laughs, walking me up the sidewalk, and leads me through his front door without saying another word. In my alcohol-addled brain, I wonder if I've made him angry for showing up drunk and uninvited. And sniffing him.

He grabs my purse from my hand and tosses it onto the couch before turning to look at me. His eyes take me in from head to toe and he whistles.

"Jesus, you're beautiful. That dress . . . fuck me, that dress," he says.

My heart soars and my body heats up at his words.

"Why are you still wearing pants?" I whisper, walking up to him and sliding my hands up his chest.

He laughs, skimming the tips of his fingers over my cleavage. Goose bumps break out on my skin and I close my eyes.

I quickly realize that was not a wise move. The room starts to spin and my stomach churns. I feel his lips on my neck and I quickly open my eyes, forcing the nausea back down.

He kisses his way up the side of my neck and the tip of his tongue traces a small circle right behind my ear. I'm torn between the need I feel for him and the need to throw up. I'm not really sure right now which one is going to win.

Dallas pulls his face away from the side of my neck and stares into my eyes. I try really hard to focus on him, but I'm not sure which "him" to look at. Right now I see three.

"Do you have any idea how hard it is not to strip you naked right now?" he whispers.

"The dress has a zipper on the side—it's not that hard," I tell him.

He chuckles and cups my face in his hands. "I'd prefer it if you were a little more coherent the first time I take you."

I want to tell him that's the hottest thing anyone has ever said to me. I want to tell him that I've never ached for anyone as much as I do him. I want to tell him so many things and they're all swirling around in my brain begging to be let out.

But instead, I just pat my hand against his cheek.

"I think I'm going to throw up."

He takes a step back and points down the hall. I cover my mouth and make a mad dash for the bathroom.

Whoever thought getting drunk was a good idea should be shot.

CHAPTER 16

R olling over with a sigh, I snuggle my body closer to the warmth in my bed. I slide my hand across smooth skin and briefly wonder if Kennedy shaved Snowball when I wasn't looking. Slowly opening my eyes, I glance across the pillow and see Dallas smiling at me.

"HOLY SHIT!"

Scrambling away from him, I move to the edge of the bed and sit up, the action causing my brain to feel like it's going to explode. Squinting my eyes to try and make the pain go away, I stare at his body, naked from the waist up. Looking down at myself quickly, I see that I have a T-shirt on.

"Where's my dress?"

Dallas raises his arm and points to the corner of the room. My dress is draped over the back of the chair and my shoes are on the floor next to it.

Oh, my God. Did we have sex? Why can't I remember? And why does it feel like someone kicked me in the head?

I reach my hand up and rest it on my forehead.

"There's aspirin and a glass of water on the nightstand next to you," he says casually as he pushes himself up to lean against the headboard.

I hear his words, but I can't process them. All I can do is stare at his naked chest and all of the ink on his arms. Unfortunately, my head is screaming at me to do something. I turn my gaze away from Dallas, and down the pills and the entire glass of water.

Setting the glass back down, I find him staring at me. I'm sure I look super this morning. I drank so much I didn't take my hair down or wash off my makeup. I probably look like a circus clown.

"Did I . . . I mean, did we . . ." I trail off, pointing between the two of us.

He laughs and shakes his head at me. "No. No, we did not. I'm going to make us some breakfast. I think I have an extra toothbrush and stuff in the bathroom if you want to shower."

He slides out of bed and I stare at his back while he pulls a pair of jeans on over his black boxer briefs. Thank God we didn't have sex last night. That's something I would like to remember.

"Did you change my clothes for me?"

If he saw me naked while I was completely obliterated, I will be mortified.

"Don't worry; I didn't look. I pulled one of my T-shirts on over your dress and you did the rest yourself. I was going to let you sleep in here and crash on the couch, but with the amount of liquor you threw up in my toilet, I figured I'd better sleep next to you and make sure you didn't die," he tells me with a laugh as he walks from the room.

Scratch that. I would have preferred his seeing me naked rather than everything else he had to witness. I don't know whether to feel grateful that he took such good care of me and didn't take advantage or a little miffed. It would have been nice to know he at least *wanted* to look. Liquid courage failed me in more ways than one.

Dragging myself out of bed, I head to Dallas's bathroom and take the hottest shower I can, scrubbing off last night's makeup and drunken humiliation. When I get out, I see that Dallas left another one of his T-shirts and a pair of his boxers on the bed for me to wear. I glance over at my dress in the corner and wonder if I should just slip that back on and leave so I don't have to face him again.

The smell of bacon and eggs permeates the room and my stomach growls. It would be rude to just leave now when he's making me breakfast. And I guess I should be happy he didn't take advantage of me in my inebriated state last night.

Quickly slipping on the shirt and boxers before I change my mind, I run my fingers through my damp hair and make my way out into the kitchen. I pause in the doorway, watching the way the muscles in Dallas's back move as he works around the kitchen, stirring food and pulling plates out of the cabinet.

It takes everything in me not to walk up behind him and run my hands up his naked back to feel those muscles under my fingers.

I clear my throat so I don't startle him. He turns around with a spatula in his hand and pauses as he looks at me. I nervously pull at the hem of his shirt. It's huge on me, but I'm still conscious of the fact that I'm not wearing a bra. I didn't need one with the dress I wore to the wedding.

"You look good in my clothes," he says softly as he sets the spatula down on the counter and walks over to me.

"Look, I'm sorry about last night. I shouldn't have come over here like that. I never drink, especially not that much."

Dallas reaches up and runs his fingers through my hair.

"What do you want, Lorelei?" he asks softly.

I swallow and stare up at him. He's looking at me imploringly, like he wants me to say something that will change everything. To admit what I'm feeling in the bright light of day without the haze of alcohol clouding my brain and my heart. I suddenly want more than anything to just let go; throw caution to the wind and not worry about the consequences. With a deep breath, I take the plunge.

"You. I just want you."

A smile spreads across his face and he shrugs. "You already have me. If you want more, just take it."

Paige was right. He wants me to make the next move. Moving quickly before I lose my nerve, I reach down and grab the hem of his shirt I'm wearing, pulling it up and off my body. I toss it onto the kitchen floor and watch Dallas's eyes darken with need as he stares at me. Sliding my fingers into the waistband of his boxers, I push them down my legs and step out of them.

"Fuck, you are so beautiful," he groans.

I take a step toward him and run my hands up his chest. He sucks in a breath and closes his eyes. "Does this mean you don't want breakfast first?"

I slide one hand down the front of him and inch my fingers into the waistband of his jeans. I tug on them roughly and haul him up against me.

"Fuck breakfast," I tell him with a smile.

His lips are on mine immediately. I wrap my arms around his shoulders and his hands go to my ass, pulling me up off of the floor so I can wrap my legs around his hips. As his tongue swirls around mine, he walks me backward and then sets me down on top of the kitchen table.

I reach between us and unsnap his jeans, helping him slide them and his boxers down his hips. While he's busy taking them the rest of the way off, my hand wraps around his hard length and I slowly slide my hand from base to tip, over and over.

He moans roughly into my mouth as he deepens the kiss. I clutch tightly onto handfuls of his hair as his palms skim up the inside of my thighs. My legs tighten around his hips and I continue working him over with my hand. My movements pause when I feel the tips of his fingers against my center. Pulling my mouth away from his, I moan softly when he slides his fingers through my wetness.

"Jesus, you always feel amazing," he mutters, resting his forehead against mine.

I move my hand away from him and grab on to his shoulder for support. He slides one hand around to cup my ass and pull me closer to the edge of the table and at the same time, he plunges two fingers inside of me. I let out a gasp and he swallows my cries with his mouth. He touches me the same way he's always kissed me—a delicious blend of rough and gentle. He knows exactly how and where to touch me and it's like he instinctively knows what I've been missing all my adult life. I want to be taken. I want the mixture of pain and pleasure.

He slides his thumb back and forth over my clit as his fingers move inside me. I thrust my hips against his hand as he pushes me closer and closer to the edge. His mouth leaves mine and he makes a trail of kisses across my cheek and to the side of my neck. Just like the night before, the tip of his tongue traces a circle right behind my ear. His fingers move harder and faster against me and I cling tightly to him as my orgasm rushes through me.

I whimper and moan through my release, clutching tightly to Dallas as he pulls every bit of pleasure out of my body.

I'm not ready for this feeling to be over. I want more. I need more. I need all of him right now.

Grabbing onto his hips, I pull him closer to me.

"I need you; I need you," I chant against his lips.

"Condoms are in the bedroom," he whispers.

Sliding one hand around his erection and clutching onto his ass with the other, I pull him against me. "I'm on the pill. Fuck the condoms."

Dallas groans as the tip of his penis slides into me. "Jesus Christ, woman. You're going to be the death of me with that mouth."

I smile as he holds himself still, barely inside me. "Just shut up and fuck me already."

He cuts off my words with his mouth, pulls his hips back, and slams into me.

The table legs scrape across the floor with the force of his movements. I wrap my arms and legs tightly around him as he takes me. With each rough thrust of his hips, I feel another orgasm building. I love the feel of his hands roughly clutching my ass and I know there will be bruises there tomorrow. I love how he isn't gentle with me and nips at the side of my neck with his teeth. I love how perfectly our bodies fit together.

As another orgasm rushes through me, I clutch Dallas, and he follows right behind me, shouting my name during his release. As we cling to each other and try to catch our breaths, it occurs to me just how many things I love about him. With all of the changes I've made in my life lately, the one thing I never expected to alter was my opinion on falling in love again.

CHAPTER 17

A few hours later, I'm lying in Dallas's bed on my stomach with my arms tucked under my head after another round of amazing sex. I feel his fingers lightly tracing the words of the tattoo on the side of my ribs.

"I take it back. You saying 'fuck' is pretty hot, but seeing this ink on your skin is hotter. What made you get this saying?"

I turn my head on the pillow to face him. "You've met my parents. I think it's pretty obvious why I got it."

He nods and reads the words out loud. "I will never give up. I will never look back. I will live my life."

Just hearing those words puts a smile on my face. Contrary to what I told my parents, I never told Steve Burdick to shove the partnership up his ass. I did, however, tell him I was taking a leave of absence. He wasn't happy at all, but I couldn't let that bother me. I wanted to be able to put my full efforts into this investigation and I couldn't do that with my caseload.

"I heard a song on the radio and I liked the words," I explain to him.

He leans down and places a kiss against my tattoo. "They're good words. They fit you."

My cell phone rings on the bedside table and I lean over to grab it. Seeing that it's Doug, I give Dallas a sheepish look and quickly answer.

"Hey, what's up? Aren't you supposed to be on your honeymoon?"

"We're on our way to the airport right now, but I had to call you," Doug answers. "Remember when I told you I'd ask around about Miles and whether or not he is a friend of Dorothy's?"

I laugh and shake my head. "Sure. But you know this could have waited until next week, right?"

"Oh please! Gossip this juicy needs to be shared!" Doug tells me. "It seems our fellow alum was caught with a fellow. One of Gary's friends from the restaurant was working a fund-raiser last year. He walked into the bathroom and found Miles on his knees with one of the other waitstaff."

To say I'm shocked is an understatement. Miles really is gay.

I thank Doug and wish him well on his honeymoon before hanging up. Getting out of Dallas's bed, I pull on my dress and explain to him about the phone call and about what Doug told me the night before about Richard.

"We need to go back and talk to Stephanie again. Ask her if she knew anything about her husband being gay. That would definitely push any woman over the edge," Dallas says with a laugh.

I pause in putting on my shoes to stare at him angrily.

"Did you really just say that?"

He stops laughing and looks at me in confusion for a few seconds before the smile is wiped from his face. "Oh, fuck. I'm sorry! I didn't mean that the way it came out. Of course *you* wouldn't do something like that. But she might."

His backpedaling does nothing to soothe my irritation.

He quickly gets out of bed and reaches for his jeans, sliding them up his legs. "I want to see Stephanie again and gauge her reaction to the news."

And now I'm jealous. I hate this feeling! This is why I didn't want to get involved with anyone ever again.

"Of course, you want to see Stephanie again. Would you like me to leave you alone so you can take her out for another round of drinks?" I ask sarcastically.

He finishes buttoning his pants and walks around the bed to me. "I didn't sleep with Stephanie."

"I didn't say you did," I huff as I zip up my dress.

He reaches out and helps me with the zipper. "You didn't have to. I can see it all over your face."

"It's none of my business if you did," I tell him with a roll of my eyes.

He puts his hands on my cheeks and turns my face to him. "What just happened here makes it your business."

His words make me want to melt. And take my dress back off, get into bed with him, and forget the outside world. But I can't do that. I need to be strong and not get pulled under by a man like Dallas. He has the power to break me. I already trust him with my life; I'm not ready to trust him with my heart.

"I need to go home and feed my cat. We can talk about this later," I tell him, pulling away from his hands.

"When did you get a cat?" he asks as he follows me to the door.

"I probably shouldn't tell you that right now. I may or may not have done something illegal to get her," I admit.

He laughs and holds the door open for me. "We're okay here, right?"

I stare up at him and put on a smile. "Yep, we're fine. I'll call you later and we can go talk to Stephanie."

Dallas kisses me one last time before I go. As I walk to the cab waiting in the driveway, I wonder if I made a mistake by forcing Dallas to work with me. I should have stuck to my guns and done it on my own. I like my independence. I like being able to come and go as I please. I finally get out from under my parents' thumb and then I go right under the watchful eye of someone else.

But Dallas is nothing like my parents; I know that now. He's much worse. If whatever this is between us doesn't work out, I'll never survive telling him off and walking away. Maybe some distance to clear my head right now will do me some good. All of this is just moving too fast. A few weeks ago I couldn't stand him. Now I'm getting jealous and hating the idea of being away from him. And how do I really know that he isn't just doing all of this as a way to keep an eye on his investigation?

———

After a quick change of clothes at my place, I go up to the office to start making calls. First, I call a few colleagues from my law firm who know Miles. I ask them if they have heard anything about his being gay. Most of them are shocked by my question and adamantly deny ever hearing any such rumor. However, a few of them say it was a definite possibility. My next few calls are to some acquaintances of Stephanie's. I didn't want to call any of her close friends for fear that it would get back to her. I call people who worked with her on charity events and a few random people whose names were given to me when I talked to the individuals who worked with her, like the woman who used to do her hair and the cleaning service she uses for her home. None of them have ever heard Stephanie say anything about Richard being gay. They do, however, tell me in great detail about the porn addiction Stephanie claimed he had.

It's dark out by the time I finish with all of my calls and type up my notes. I check my phone and see that I've missed five calls from Dallas. With a sigh, I slide my phone into my purse without calling him back.

On the drive to my house, I call my mother to check on her. Since Doug's wedding the other night, she's called me no less than ten times to give me updates on her "new" life.

"I'm wearing jeans and a T-shirt, Lorelei. Isn't that exciting?" she asks as I pull off of the exit on the highway.

I laugh and shake my head. "That's amazing. How's Dad?"

"I don't know and I don't care. He tried apologizing, and when I asked him what he was apologizing for, he had no idea. So I slammed the door in his face. I think I'm going to take a lover. Do people still call it that nowadays?" she asks.

Am I really having this conversation with my mother right now?

"Mom, I think you and Dad need to talk before you do anything too rash."

She ignores me. "How is Dallas? Did you tell him I was sorry for being so rude at dinner?"

The last time she called me I was naked in bed with him. My thoughts cloud with the memory of his lips on my neck and his hands on my hips.

I shake my head to clear my thoughts. "Yes, I told him. It's fine."

"He's a nice young man. And he's very good-looking. You should sleep with him."

I choke on a laugh at the words coming out of her mouth.

"Don't laugh. I'm serious. I wish I had slept with more men before I married your father," she tells me.

"Okay, well, I'm hanging up now. I just got home. I'll call you tomorrow," I tell her as I pull into the driveway and shut off my car.

"Don't call before noon. I have an appointment with a tattoo artist."

I drop my keys and my phone almost slips from my hand as I get out of the car. "What?! Mom, are you serious?"

"They looked so nice on Dallas. And you said you had one. I want to do something exciting too," she tells me.

"Oh, my God," I mutter, as I grab my keys from the ground and make my way up to my door. "This is a little too much for me right now. I'll talk to you tomorrow."

"Okay, sweetie. Wish me luck!"

I end the call with a shake of my head. Unlocking the door, I push it open. Just as I start to turn around to close the door behind me, something slams into my shoulder, shoving me the rest of the way into the house.

My keys, purse, and phone fly out of my hand and clatter to the floor as my body takes another hit, this one hard enough to make me lose my footing, and I slam against the ground. The wind is knocked out of me and I wheeze, trying to take in a lungful of air. Once the shock of what is happening wears off, I push and shove at the weight on top of me, pinning me to the ground. In the dark entryway of my house, I can just make out a face with a black ski mask. Fear and panic ripple through me as I twist and turn, trying to get out of the person's grasp. I see a hand come up and before I can move my head out of the way, a fist slams into my cheek.

I see stars for a few seconds and all of the self-defense training Kennedy taught me rushes through my mind. My elbow flies up and connects with the person's eye and I hear a shocked gasp of pain. I take that opportunity to buck my hips and shove him off of me. When I'm free from the weight of the intruder's body, I flip over onto my belly and stumble up to my feet. No sooner do I stand up than a hand clamps around both my ankles and yanks my feet backward, forcing me back onto the ground. I immediately flop onto my back and kick out as hard as I can. My foot connects against the person's mouth and he falls back, his head smacking against the floor with a thunk.

Scrambling backward on my butt, I quickly grab my purse and pull out the Taser. Flipping on the switch, I hear the Taser crackle to life as the voltage lights up the room.

The masked figure doesn't move for a few seconds as he contemplates his next move. Before I can say anything, the person jumps up and races out the front door.

With a shaking hand, I grab my phone from the floor and dial.

CHAPTER 18

O ne of the officers brings me some ice wrapped in a towel from my kitchen and hands it to me.

Ted sighs and gets up from his spot on the couch next to me. I look up at him as I press the towel of ice to my cheek. "So, just some random mugging. Are you sure there isn't anything you're leaving out?"

Oh, there's a whole bunch I'm leaving out, but I don't want you to throw me in jail.

I know sharing the information we have with the police would move the investigation forward, but if I do that, I'm not only putting myself in jeopardy, but Dallas as well. He went out on a limb by letting me help with this case. Even though my head and my heart are in knots right now, I'm not about to get him in trouble.

"I'm sure. I heard that there have been some break-ins around here lately. I'm sure that's what it was. Unfortunately for him, your sister taught me some wonderful self-defense moves," I tell him.

"And thank God for that. Are you sure you want to stay here tonight? There's no shame in going somewhere else until we can get a bead on this guy," Ted tells me.

"I'm not going to be forced out of my home. I'm staying here," I tell him adamantly.

Besides, at this point, it could only be one of two people who did this. I made a lot of phone calls today about Stephanie and Miles. I'm guessing one of them found out about it.

Ted sighs as he shoves his small notepad into the inside pocket of his suit coat. "Fine. But I'm stationing an officer in a patrol car outside for the rest of the night."

Before I can argue, I hear Dallas's voice from the doorway. "That won't be necessary. I'm going to stay here with her tonight."

Seeing him standing in my house, so large and looking more than a little ticked off, all of the adrenaline coursing through my body since the attack leaves me in a whoosh. I suddenly want nothing more than to run over to him and have him wrap his arms around me.

Ted looks back and forth between us. "Lorelei, this okay with you?"

I drop the hand holding the ice to my face and nod. Dallas's eyes narrow when he sees the bruise that I'm sure is forming on my cheek. It feels like it's on fire and the whole side of my face aches, so I'm sure it looks less than pleasant.

"All right then; we're done here. If you can think of anything else, give me a call. I'll just need you to stop by the station some time tomorrow to sign the report once we get it typed up," Ted tells me.

Dallas doesn't take his eyes off of me as Ted walks up to him and smacks him on the back before walking out the door. The other officer follows him, closing the door behind himself.

I can hear the tick of the clock hanging on the wall above my head. In the quiet of my house with Dallas standing so far away and looking like he's about ready to punch the wall, I finally lose the battle of trying to be strong. My eyes grow blurry with tears and I look away from Dallas as they fall.

He's next to me on the couch in an instant, wrapping me in his arms and pulling me against him. I sink into him and let myself cry. He runs the palm of his hand down the back of my head over and over as he rocks me slowly back and forth. When I'm all cried out, I pull away from him, wiping the tears off of my face and wincing when my fingers brush over the bruise on the side of my cheek. Dallas picks up the towel with ice in my hand and presses it gently against my cheek.

"I'm going to kill whoever did this to you," he mutters, brushing a strand of hair off the other side of my face.

"I'm pretty sure I know who it is."

He pulls back to look at my eyes. "Does this have anything to do with why you wouldn't return my calls all day?"

I sigh, taking the towel out of his hand and holding it myself. "I'm sorry about that. I should have called you back. I just . . . I don't know how to do this."

He looks at me in confusion. "How to do what?"

"This! You and me. Whatever *this* is. I finally stood up to my parents and I'm doing something for me. I just went to my ex-husband's wedding. I don't know how to do all of that and deal with what's going on with us at the same time."

Dallas slides off of the couch and gets down on his knees in front of me, resting his hands on top of my thighs.

"You don't have to *deal* with anything involving us. I don't know what this is either, but I'm not about to walk away from it."

The tears are back again, this time pouring out of me so quickly that I don't even bother trying to swipe them away. Dallas reaches up and does it for me.

"Other than the shiner on your face, are you hurt anywhere else?" he asks.

I shrug and take a few deep breaths. "My shoulder and my hip are killing me from when he slammed me into the floor, but it's probably just bruises."

A look of pure fury washes over Dallas's face when I casually mention this and I quickly try to calm him. "Don't worry; I got a few good hits in. He took an elbow to the eye and a kick to the face."

Just then, Snowball races into the room and right up to Dallas. I cringe, waiting for her to bare her teeth and hiss at him, but she just sniffs his jeans and then sits back on her hind legs.

He reaches down and scratches her behind her ears. She purrs and rubs her face against his hand.

"Are you kidding me? I rescued you from a life of loneliness and all you've done is hiss at me since I brought you home. You are such a hussy," I tell her in annoyance. Of course she turns and hisses at me before going right back and rubbing herself all over Dallas.

I kind of don't blame her. If I weren't in so much pain right now, I'd be doing the same thing.

Dallas laughs and reaches down, scooping her up into his arms and holding her at arm's length in front of him.

"Why does this cat look familiar?" he asks.

I wipe the irritated look off of my face and stare down at the towel in my lap, pretending I'm fascinated with the flower design.

"Oh, my God. Did you take this cat from Covington's house? Oh Jesus, that's where you guys got the e-mails too, isn't it?" he asks.

"Hey, you were being a total jerk at the time. I had to do something to get the upper hand. And besides, it was Kennedy's idea," I tell him lamely.

He shakes his head with a hint of a smile. "It's good to know I was completely wrong about you at first. You do have balls. And by the way, so does your cat."

He turns Snowball around and she hisses at me. I mean, *he* hisses at me.

"That could be why he hates you. You've been calling 'him' a 'her.' I'd be pissed at that too," he says with a laugh.

He sets Snowball down and we watch as he runs off to another room.

"So, let me guess? Stephanie or Miles?" he asks, running his fingers gently over the bruise on my cheek.

I sigh. "Even though they're both suspect at this point because I called around about each of them today, it had to be Miles. He was wearing a mask, but there's no way that was Stephanie. She doesn't strike me as the type of person who would—or even could—attack someone. Plus, I didn't feel her huge boobs against me when I was pinned to the ground."

Dallas chuckles. "Stephanie has huge boobs?"

I scoff and smack him in the arm. "Oh, please, like you didn't notice."

He pushes himself up off the ground and grabs my hands, pulling me up from the couch and into his arms. "Baby, I haven't looked at anyone's boobs since the first time you insulted me."

After what he just said to me a little bit ago, I actually believe him. Wrapping my arms around his waist, I press the unbruised side of my face against his chest.

"Come on, let's get you to bed. We've got a lot of work to do tomorrow."

As he leads me down the hall to my room, it hits me that I might just be falling in love with Dallas Osborne.

CHAPTER 19

D allas didn't want to leave me alone this morning, but he said he had a meeting about another case he had to handle quickly and I promised him that I would call him immediately if I saw anyone suspicious.

I know he trusts that I can take care of myself, but it's kind of nice to have someone worry about me. After a quick phone call to my mom, I find out she didn't go through with the tattoo. At least that's something I don't have to worry about right now.

I didn't want to bother Kennedy with what happened because I knew she was away with Griffin and quite possibly getting proposed to. As I get in my car to head to the police station to finish the report, I check the clock and figure she's probably home by now.

"Why the hell didn't you call me last night?" she answers.

"Well, hello to you too," I reply with a laugh.

"This is serious, Lorelei. Someone came into your home. Whose ass do I need to kick?" she asks.

"You'll be happy to know that I did just fine kicking some ass on my own," I tell her.

"Did you use the eye gouge and the head butt?" she asks excitedly.

I laugh at her exuberance. "No. I used my elbow to his eye and my foot to his face."

Kennedy sighs. "I think I'm going to cry."

"Enough about me; how did it go with Griffin? Did he pop the question?" I ask.

All joking aside, when she speaks next, I really do think I hear tears in her voice. "He did. It was so romantic. It was first and ten and Notre Dame had the ball. He passed me a can of cheddar cheese Pringles and the ring was at the bottom."

Only Kennedy would think that was romantic.

I congratulate her and tell her to make up a story that includes flowers and a string quartet to tell Paige, otherwise *she'll* be the one crying.

Pulling into the police station, I can't keep the smile off of my face as I make my way through the doors. Regardless of how the evening started off last night, it ended pretty well. We're getting close to finishing this investigation.

I wave to a few of the officers as I make my way to the front desk to ask for Ted. I have to come in here a lot to file reports for Fool Me Once and also to speak to officers for my court cases, so I know pretty much everyone in here by now.

"Hey, Lorelei. Ted said you'd be stopping by to finish that report."

I smile at one of the younger officers as I step up to the front desk. "Is he here?"

He nods and points down the hall behind him. "Yep, he's in his office. You can go on in."

I tell him thanks and head off down the hall. As I get closer, I can hear Ted's voice talking to someone. I slow down and listen for a second. If he's in with someone else, I'll just go back out to the lobby and wait until he's finished. I start to turn around and head back down the hall when another voice makes me pause.

"I swear—I'm making sure nothing gets screwed up," Dallas says.

My heartbeat speeds up. I know I should just continue back to the lobby, but something keeps me rooted in place.

"I don't like this at all, Dallas. I've got people up my ass wanting this case solved," Ted replies.

"Believe me, I don't like it any more than you do. Obviously she doesn't know what the hell she's doing. Look what happened last night," Dallas tells him.

What's that supposed to mean? Someone attacked me and I fought back.

"She wasn't supposed to be anywhere near this case," Ted complains.

"I know, and she's not. Not really. I just let her believe that. Why do you think I've been spending so much time with her? I don't want this screwed up any more than you do," Dallas answers.

I gasp and my hand flies up to cover my mouth.

"I trust that you know what you're doing and that you'll solve this case. Just get it done. The faster you find out who killed Richard Covington, the sooner you'll be able to stop babysitting my sister's friend."

Both men laugh and I squeeze my eyes closed to keep the tears at bay. They move on to other topics like sports and the weather. I turn and run back the way I came.

The officer at the front desk calls to me as I race past. Swiping angrily at the tears, I compose myself before I turn to face him.

"Hey, we just got a report in from the ME's office on the Covington investigation. I know I'm not supposed to show this to civilians, but I heard you were working with Osborne on this thing. You want to look at it before I hand it over to him?" he asks.

Sucking up my wounded pride, I walk back to the desk and grab the report from his hand. Scanning through the pages, my eyes zero in on the section showing the traces of particulates that were found on Richard's clothes. My jaw drops when I see one unusual item in particular. I thank the officer and quickly hand the file back to him, exiting the police station before Dallas and Ted realize I've been there.

Starting up my car, I quickly back out of my parking space and peel out of the lot. Dallas won't have to worry about "babysitting" me for much longer. I just solved this case and he can kiss my ass when he finds out I did it on my own.

———

Pulling into Stephanie Covington's driveway, I take a few deep breaths to calm my nerves as I walk up to her front door and ring the bell.

The door is swung open moments later and my mouth drops open in shock. Standing in front of me isn't Stephanie, but a very butch-looking woman. She's a few inches taller than me, with short, spiky blond hair and enough muscles to make a bodybuilder jealous. That isn't what has me momentarily speechless, though. The black eye and busted lip she's currently sporting does.

"Aw, shit," she mutters.

Before I can react, she grabs on to my arm and hauls me into the house, slamming the door closed behind her.

She drags me into the living room and pushes me onto the couch.

"You! You're the one who attacked me last night. Who the hell *are* you?" I ask, standing back up from the couch.

She stalks over to me and places her hands on my chest, shoving me down again.

"Sit there and shut up. I need to think," she tells me angrily.

"YOU need to think? Screw you! Are you covering for Stephanie? Did she hire you to come to my house because she killed her husband and she knows I'm onto her?" I fire at her.

"Sweetie, your tea's getting cold."

I look up as Stephanie walks into the room, stopping in her tracks when she sees me there. "Oh, dear."

Standing up from the couch again, I shoot the crazy, manhandling woman a dirty look before she can shove me back down.

"Mel, what did you do?" Stephanie asks, turning to the woman currently glaring at me.

"She attacked me in my home last night. And you killed your ex-husband, so you're both going to jail," I tell her.

"What?! I didn't kill Richard! What are you talking about? Mel, what is she talking about?" Stephanie asks, turning to this Mel person.

"Oh, cut the bullshit, Stephanie. The medical examiner's report is in. They found traces of taheebo bark all over Richard's shirt the day he was killed. If I remember correctly, you drink taheebo tea, don't you?"

Stephanie glances down at the cup of tea in her hand and quickly sets it down on an end table. She looks back and forth between Mel and me nervously.

"Oh, Mel, tell me you didn't?" Stephanie whispers.

Mel sighs and walks over to Stephanie, placing her hands on her shoulders.

"Baby, I had to do something. He was gonna shut down my business and tell everyone about us. I couldn't let that happen."

What the hell is going on right now?

I watch in strange fascination as the two of them embrace. Stephanie pulls away first and looks over at me.

"Lori, this is my herbalist and . . . lover, Melinda. She really didn't mean to do this. Can't we just pretend like it never happened? I mean, you're just a reporter. You could say I wouldn't comment or something, can't you?" she begs.

"I'm not a reporter and my name's not Lori Wagner. It's Lorelei Warner and I'm a private investigator. I was hired to solve Richard's murder," I explain.

Well, technically I was only hired to deliver a subpoena to Richard for their divorce. She doesn't need to know I coerced my way into solving Richard's murder with a man I thought I was falling in love with and thinks I'm worthless when it comes to this job. Those are just silly little details when I'm standing in front of a murderer and her accomplice.

"What? You lied to me? How DARE you!" Stephanie shouts. "I can't believe this. I even had Mel put together some herbs for you and run your astrology chart. Your third house is in Neptune, by the way, which means your rational mind is going to try and deceive you in your pursuit of the truth in your heart."

I have no idea what she's blathering on about. Ignoring her, I reach into my back pocket for my cell phone to call the police. As soon as I pull it out, Melinda smacks it out of my hand.

"What the hell are you doing?" I scream at her, moving to pick up my phone.

As I bend down, I hear the click of a bullet being loaded into the chamber of a gun. I pause, and lift my head slowly to see Melinda aiming a gun at my face.

"Melinda! Put that away! You know how I hate guns. They completely mess with my aura. I feel a headache coming on," Stephanie complains.

"Yes, listen to Stephanie. How about you put the gun away and we can talk?" I tell her, trying not to freak out that there is a loaded gun aimed right at me.

"What's there to talk about? I love Stephanie and she loves me," Melinda says with a shrug. "Her loser of an ex-husband found out about us and was gonna tell everyone. It didn't matter that he only married her so no one would know he was gay and that the affair he was having was with another dude, his secretary, no less. He said if I didn't leave town for good, he'd have my business shut down. I didn't want Stephanie's reputation ruined, and without my business we wouldn't have any money. So I went over there one day and got rid of the asshole. "

Well, that explains Stephanie's anger when she walked in on Richard having sex with his secretary. I suddenly feel her pain.

Stephanie covers her heart with her hand. "Melinda, I can't believe you did this."

Melinda turns to look at her and nods. "I might as well tell you I killed Andrew Jameson too. Richard told me right before I shot him that Andrew knew all about us. He confided in Andrew back when they were still friends, before Richard fired him. I'd been keeping an eye on him for a few days and it seemed like he was too busy drinking to care. But then this one showed up at his house and I knew he would tell her," Melinda says angrily, pointing in my direction. "You probably hate me now, huh?"

Stephanie shakes her head back and forth frantically before running up to Melinda and throwing her arms around her. "I could never hate you! That's the most romantic thing anyone has ever done for me."

With the gun still aimed at me, Melinda wraps one arm around Stephanie's waist and plants a passionate kiss on her lips.

"If you knew about Richard, what was the point of telling everyone he had a porn addiction? Wouldn't it have just been easier to tell everyone he was gay?" I ask Stephanie.

She pulls away from Melinda and shrugs. "I was afraid. I figured if people knew about him, it would only be a matter of time before they found out about me and Mel. I wasn't ready for the world to share our love. He never had a porn addiction. I just made that up so people wouldn't find out the truth."

Right then, the front door bursts open and Dallas charges in with his gun drawn. "Drop the weapon! NOW!"

CHAPTER 20

As happy as I am to see someone else here to help me, I'm downright pissed off that it's Dallas.

Melanie turns her gun away from me and aims it at Dallas. "I'm not putting my gun down. YOU put your gun down."

Dallas takes a few careful steps into the house, glancing over at me. "You okay, baby?"

I scoff at him and roll my eyes. "Don't call me 'baby.' And while you're at it, fuck off."

He stares at me in shock and I turn away from him. Melinda shoves her gun into my ribs. I wince at the pain.

"Put your gun down or I shoot her," Melinda tells Dallas.

He puts his free hand in the air as he bends down slowly and places his gun on the floor by his feet. "I'm putting my gun down. You don't need to shoot anyone."

"But, hey, if you're in the mood, feel free to shoot him," I tell Melinda, nodding in Dallas's direction.

"Lorelei? What the fuck?" Dallas asks in confusion as he stands back up.

"I wasn't born yesterday. Kick your gun away from you," Melinda tells him.

Dallas huffs and uses the toe of his boot to slide the gun across the room.

"Now, let's have ourselves a little chat and see what we're going to do about this situation," Melinda says.

"Oh, that sounds like fun. I think he should go first. He could tell us all about how he's a lying sack of shit," I say angrily, staring at Dallas.

"What in the hell is your problem?" Dallas fires back.

"MY problem? That's rich coming from you. Hmmm, let me think." I tap my finger against my chin and pretend to contemplate. "I don't know what I'm doing, you only slept with me to make sure I didn't screw anything up—am I forgetting anything? Oh, that's right! The sooner you can solve this case, the sooner you can stop babysitting little old me."

The anger on Dallas's face melts away and he closes his eyes.

Melinda whistles next to me. "Wow, that's pretty low, dude."

Dallas sighs and finally opens his eyes, ignoring Melinda and looking right at me. "You heard Ted and me talking."

I roll my eyes at him. "Don't even think about denying it. I was standing right there."

I refuse to let the pain in my heart show. I will not be broken by another man.

"I'm not denying it. I said every word," Dallas admits.

I think my heart might actually still be intact right now if he had tried to deny it. Hearing him openly admit what he really thinks of me makes it shatter into a million pieces.

"The chakras in this room will never be the same. I'm going to have to move," Stephanie complains with a sigh. "At least your aura isn't gray anymore, Lorelei. It's a lovely shade of pink, so that means you're in love. Congratulations!"

My eyes widen and I quickly glance at Dallas, hoping he didn't hear that last part. He's staring at me with a smile.

"You're in love with me?" he asks.

"Oh, please! She has no idea what she's talking about. You can go right to hell!" I yell at him.

"I've studied auras for years. I definitely know what I'm talking about," Stephanie adds.

I roll my eyes at her and cross my arms over my chest.

"Lorelei, I didn't mean what I said to Ted. I swear," Dallas confesses.

"You expect me to believe that line of bullshit?" I shout.

"Yes, I do! After what's happened between us, I sure as fuck expect you to believe that I'm in love with you, Lorelei, and I would never do that to you," he argues back.

My jaw drops at his admission, but it doesn't change anything.

"Miles actually went to the department and said something about us working together. Ted headed him off, but he was worried the guy would just go talk to someone else. I was covering for you. I didn't mean any of those things I said to him. He suspects we've been lying to him, but as long as he's not sure, there's nothing he can do."

I shake my head and look away from him.

Could he be telling the truth? I don't know what to believe.

"Um, hello? Can we get back to the important matter at hand? I'm the one with the Goddamn gun here!" Melinda yells.

"Honey, just put the gun down. We can pack up some things and run away together," Stephanie tells her.

Melinda looks at Stephanie for a moment and then back to me. She forcefully shoves me away from her and I stumble, falling to my hands and knees in front of Dallas while she runs over to Stephanie and scoops her up in her arms.

Smacking away Dallas's outstretched hand, I push myself up from the ground and watch as Stephanie and Melinda embrace.

"Do you mean it? We can just leave and go wherever we want?" Melinda asks Stephanie excitedly.

"Holy shit, are we in a porno?" Dallas mutters next to me as he stares at Stephanie and Melinda while they kiss.

I start to laugh and then realize I'm still pissed at him. Dammit!

"I meant it, you know? I love you, Lorelei. Think with your heart and not your brain for once. You know damn well I was lying when I said all of those things to Ted," Dallas whispers. "You didn't need me to solve this case. You never needed me to look after you. You beat the shit out of your attacker last night and you solved this thing. I'm so fucking proud of you."

I bite down on my lips and refuse to look at him. I know if I look at him, I'll be lost.

"Put the gun down and we can leave right now," Stephanie tells Melinda.

There's a few feet separating Dallas and me right now and his gun is even farther away. Out of the corner of my eye, I see him slowly inching his way closer to where he kicked the gun.

Melinda suddenly looks over at him and the smile falls from her face.

"Were you going for your gun?" she asks.

Dallas just shrugs.

And then everything happens all at once. Melinda raises her gun, Dallas crouches down to spring across the floor to his own weapon, and I throw myself toward Dallas right as the thundering boom of a gun going off fills the quiet room.

My body slams into him and in his crouched position, he falls to the ground with me on top of him. Pain radiates through my body when we hit the floor and I know I must have jarred something loose from my scuffle with Melinda last night.

Dallas wraps his arms protectively around my body and rolls me onto my back, cradling me close to him as shouts fill the air and a stampede of police officers with guns drawn comes flying into the house.

Dallas lifts his head away from me and we both watch as Melinda and Stephanie are taken to the ground and handcuffed.

"You guys okay?" Ted asks as he flies into the room with his gun in front of him, heading over to the chaos across from us.

"Yep, we're good. Lorelei here just saved my ass. I'm pretty sure that proves she loves me too," Dallas tells him as he looks down at me and smiles.

I try to smile back, but I feel a little woozy. I must have slammed into Dallas a little too hard. The room is starting to spin and I blink quickly a few times to try and settle everything.

Dallas pulls away from me a little bit and I stare in shock at his shoulder.

"Oh, my God, you're bleeding. You've been shot," I mutter.

His face scrunches up in confusion and he looks down at himself. His gaze slowly makes its way back to me.

"That's not my blood," he whispers.

I watch as he quickly pushes himself off of me and his eyes widen in horror.

"TED! Get an ambulance here NOW!"

Dallas presses his hands to my shoulder and I yelp in pain.

"Ouch! Not so hard," I complain, closing my eyes.

"No, no, no. Lorelei, open your eyes, baby. Stay with me."

This feels like déjà vu. Hasn't he said this to me before? It suddenly strikes me as funny and I start to laugh. I feel drunk again. But I'm pretty sure I'm not drunk.

"I'm right here; I'm not going anywhere," I laugh. "I'm so tired. And my shoulder really hurts."

I close my eyes again and hear a flurry of activity all around me. People shouting, footsteps pounding on the floor by my head, and Dallas whispering close to my ear.

"Come on, open your eyes and tell me I'm a pompous asshole. Tell me I'm a pigheaded jerk. I don't care what you say, just talk to me. The ambulance is on its way."

I don't know what the ambulance is for, but Dallas makes me laugh.

"You're so silly. I love you. You're not that much of a pompous asshole," I tell him.

I struggle to open my eyes and look up at him. The smile he gives me is tinged with sadness.

Shame on him for being sad when I just told him I love him.

CHAPTER 21

"Wake up, sleepyhead."

The voice breaks into my dream and I groan in frustration. I was having the most amazing dream. I solved the murder case and Dallas told me he loved me.

"Don't wake her up. She's going to be pissed when she finds out the hospital threw away her Jimmy Choo boots because they had blood on them."

I groan again and try to roll over to go back to the dream but I can't move. There's something on my face that's tickling my nose, and my arms feel like they're tangled with rope.

"I'm pretty sure the hospital has already borne enough of *your* wrath for that oversight. I can't believe you told that orderly he was a waste of space that wouldn't know good shoes if they were shoved up his ass."

I want to laugh at the absurdity of the conversation happening around me, but I feel like it would hurt to laugh, for some reason.

"He said those boots were ugly and the blood enhanced them. He's lucky I didn't shove my own foot up his ass. Jimmy Choos are never ugly."

Figuring I may as well get it over with, I slowly blink open my eyes and wince at the bright light. Turning my head to the side, I see Kennedy and Paige sitting on chairs next to my bed. What are they doing in my room? And why is my room so bright?

"Where am I?"

The raspy groan of my own voice shocks me and I cough to try and clear it.

Paige immediately jumps up from her chair and rushes to the side of my bed. "I knew shoe talk would perk you right up. How do you feel?"

I swallow and clear my throat, pressing my palms down on the bed to push myself up. I yelp in pain as soon as I put weight on my left arm.

Kennedy gets up and hurries to my side, gently putting her hands on my chest and pushing me back down to the bed. "Nope, no getting up for you. Doctor's orders. Are you in pain?"

Closing my eyes and trying to get comfortable, I take stock of my body. Every muscle is achy and my left shoulder feels like it was run through a meat grinder.

"My shoulder. What's wrong with my shoulder?"

I look down and see a thick bandage wrapped around my shoulder and chest. Upon further inspection, I see an IV sticking out of my arm.

"Dude, you were shot. Do you remember anything from yesterday?" Kennedy asks, grabbing a cup of water with a straw in it and holding it to my lips.

Shot? She must be kidding.

I take a few long pulls on the straw and the cold water instantly soothes my scratchy throat.

Glancing around the room, I realize Dallas isn't here. I remember hearing him and Ted talking about me at the police station. I remember my heart breaking into a million pieces.

"I remember watching two women kiss," I mumble, letting my head flop back to the pillow.

"Kinky," Kennedy replies with a laugh. "I'm guessing that would be Stephanie Covington and Melinda Banks, unless you've been watching some girl-on-girl porn lately."

Paige smacks her in the arm. "Do you remember going to Stephanie's house to confront her about killing Richard?"

Racking my brain, I try to make the memory surface. I have a vague recollection of standing in Stephanie's living room, arguing with Dallas. And a gun pointed in his direction.

Like someone is flipping quickly through the pages of a book, everything rushes back in flashes of scenes.

"Did I really shove Dallas out of the way from being shot?" I ask.

"You did. You totally saved my ass."

Glancing over to the door, I see Dallas standing there with two cups of coffee in his hands, looking haggard and exhausted.

Kennedy and Paige walk up to him and grab the cups from his hands.

"We'll just leave you two alone. I'll go get the nurse and tell her it's time for some pain meds," Paige tells me before she and Kennedy leave the room.

Dallas slides his hands in his pockets and gives me a look. I think I told him I loved him after I'd been shot. Did it freak him out? I can't believe I said that. I have a faint memory of him telling me the same thing, but I don't know if it's my mind playing tricks on me or not.

"How are you feeling?" he asks softly, moving closer to the bed.

"Like I've been shot," I reply.

He chuckles, grabbing one of the empty chairs and sliding it closer to my bed before sitting down. I watch as he rests his elbows on the edge of the bed and folds his hands. I want him to touch me. Even though I'm confused about what all happened the day before, I feel cold in this bright room. He's so close to me, but feels so far away.

"Do you remember what happened?" he asks after a few minutes of silence.

I shrug, but the motion hurts. I try to keep the pain off of my face but it's no use. Dallas immediately reaches out and smoothes my hair off of my forehead. The feel of his warm hands against my skin makes the pain disappear.

"I remember bits and pieces. Paige and Kennedy told me a little bit," I tell him, turning my face into his palm and sighing.

"You saw the ME's report at the police station and immediately put two and two together from the particle traces on Richard's clothing. I would have never caught that," he admits. "Stephanie's herbalist, Melinda, was afraid of Richard telling everyone about her and Stephanie's relationship, so she killed him."

"What about Richard and Miles having a relationship? Was any of that true?" I ask.

"Just rumors. Supposedly, Stephanie didn't know anything about Melinda taking matters into her own hands, but that's still under investigation."

I nod and a heavy silence fills the room.

Dallas clears his throat and bites his lip with nervousness. "I know I said this yesterday, but I want to make sure this part is absolutely clear. I'm sorry about what you overheard at the police station. I swear to you, I didn't mean a damn word of it. You're better at this fucking job than I am. You have natural instincts that can't be taught. The only reason I would even think about saying you can't do this job on your own is because it kills me to think of something like this happening to you again," Dallas admits. "When you slammed into me at Stephanie's house and knocked me to the ground, all I could think about was how amazing you are."

I remember watching Melinda aim the gun in Dallas's direction and not even thinking about what I was going to do.

"I knew she was going to shoot you. All I could think about was getting you out of the way," I tell him.

"Jesus, when you told me I was bleeding and I looked down and saw the bullet hole in your shoulder, I couldn't breathe."

He takes his hand off of my face and runs it through his hair.

The short strands stand up in a mess and I realize he must have been doing that a lot recently.

"You kept closing your eyes and all I could do was sit there next to you, helpless, holding my hand to your shoulder. Promise me you'll never throw yourself in front of another bullet again. I don't know if my heart could take it."

Speaking of his heart . . .

"Did you really tell me you love me, or did I imagine that?" I whisper.

He smiles, reaching over and grabbing the hand of my arm that isn't bandaged and bringing it up to his mouth. He closes his eyes and kisses my hand.

He moves my palm to the side of his face and holds it in place before opening his eyes again and smiling at me. "You didn't imagine it. I love you."

I smile back at him and instinctively know he's telling the truth. About everything—his conversation with Ted and how he feels about me.

"Did you really mean it when you told me you loved me back, or was it just because of the blood loss?"

Hearing the wariness in his voice surprises me. Dallas has always been such a force of nature, so strong and sure of himself. Seeing him vulnerable like this tugs on my heart.

"Don't worry; the blood loss only gave me the courage to say it out loud," I tell him with a smile.

He gets up from the chair and leans forward, pressing his lips to mine.

"You did it, baby. You solved a murder," he tells me happily as he pulls away and looks at me.

I did, didn't I? It feels good to know I made the right decision with my life for once. I took a gamble and it paid off. Sure, I got shot in the process, but I found Richard's killer and fell in love all at the same time.

"Oh, your mom stopped by earlier. She apologized again for being a bitch to me at dinner. What is going on with her? She seems like a completely different person. It's a little scary," Dallas says.

The nurse walks in the room then and sticks a needle into my IV, letting me know the pain I'm feeling will be gone in seconds and to call her if I need anything.

"My mother is going through a phase," I tell him with a smile as the nurse leaves the room, remembering the words my mother said to me about my hair at dinner.

"I think it's more than a phase. She asked me if I had any cute single friends." Dallas laughs with a shake of his head.

I feel the medicine coursing through my veins and a pleasant, numb feeling takes over my body. My head feels heavy and my eyes start to droop. All in all, getting shot was worth it.

"Sleep, baby. I'll be here when you wake up. I love you," Dallas whispers.

Letting my eyes close, I feel his lips against my cheek and I allow the pain medication to pull me under.

Before I doze off, I hear the faint sound of Dallas's voice one more time.

"Don't be mad, but I'm never letting you out of my sight, ever again," he whispers.

Shame on him for thinking I'd be mad about that now.

EPILOGUE

Three months later . . .

"C an you idiots all shut up for a minute; I need to make my speech," Kennedy tells the room loudly.

Everyone stops talking and stares at her. She holds up her champagne glass and we all do the same. Just like usual, all of our friends and family are gathered in the office of Fool Me Once Investigations to toast to the end of another case.

Stephanie and Melinda were both arrested for the murder of Richard Covington, but Melinda immediately confessed to everything. She reiterated the fact that Stephanie knew nothing of her plans and that she was completely innocent. It took a few days for the police to verify her statements, and after that, Stephanie was free to go.

Melinda is still in jail awaiting trial and last I heard, Stephanie wasn't planning on ever visiting her. Something about the drab color of the jail putting the third star of Jupiter in her energy field. Since the story of Richard's murder being solved made the news, Stephanie had no choice but to come out of the closet. Unfortunately for Melinda, she'll be waiting a long time for Stephanie to ever thank her for clearing her name. Stephanie is now dating a nutritionist from her gym named Wendy.

The board of directors from Richard's company was so pleased with the speed with which the case was solved that it decided to foot the bill for the police department and upon my insistence, Dallas and I split the fee right down the middle.

Looking over at my friends, I see the diamond engagement ring sparkling on Kennedy's finger as Griffin puts his arm around her shoulders. Paige and Matt have their arms around each other too. Kennedy's brothers, Ted and Bobby, are sitting at Paige's desk and mine with their feet on top of them. Kennedy's father, Buddy, and her uncle Wally are bickering with each other in the corner, and Paige's mom and Matt's dad are holding hands, sitting on a couple of chairs by the front door.

My mom, wearing a pair of jeans and a Harvard Law sweatshirt, sits on the edge of Kennedy's desk, well into her third glass of champagne and starting to get a little giggly.

And me, I'm sitting on Dallas's lap with his arms wrapped firmly around me. I'm surrounded by the people I love and I couldn't be happier.

"Congratulations to Lorelei for proving she is the biggest badass out of all of us!" Kennedy announces with a smile.

Everyone laughs and lifts their glasses of champagne up a little higher.

"Who knew that almost a year ago when I met these two light-weights in a self-defense class, we would become best friends and open a pretty kick-ass private investigation firm?" Kennedy says.

"Hey, who are you calling lightweight?" Paige shouts. "I brought down a crime ring and Lorelei took a bullet. All you did was chase around a yappy dog and a freak who believes in aliens."

Everyone laughs again and I feel Dallas clasp me tighter. I lean back against his chest and smile.

"Oh, shut up!" Kennedy tells Paige. "I just want to say I'm glad that I met both of you. Here's to Fool Me Once Investigations—the best PI agency around."

Everyone cheers and takes a sip of their champagne. The loud conversations and laughter start up again.

"How's your shoulder?" Dallas asks.

I turn around on his lap to face him. "It's good. It's not sore right now."

The bullet I took to the shoulder went clean through and luckily didn't nick an artery. After my surgery, I spent three days in the hospital recuperating, and Dallas spent every single moment there with me. He also accompanied me to every physical therapy session and kept the promise he whispered to me in the hospital—he never lets me out of his sight. My shoulder still gives me a little bit of trouble every now and then, but it's manageable. The doctor said I'll be as good as new in no time.

"Good. Tomorrow we're going to the shooting range. You're going to learn how to really shoot a gun," he tells me.

He's been saying this to me ever since I got out of the hospital. I officially quit my job with the law firm and I'm now a full-time investigator. Dallas knows that eventually he won't be able to shadow me everywhere, and he told me he'd feel much better about that if he knew I could protect myself even better.

I haven't told him yet that I'm probably a better shot than he is. My father was an award-winning skeet shooter. He took me shooting every weekend for almost my entire life. Thinking about my father makes me a little sad. I haven't spoken to him since that night at dinner. He sent flowers to the hospital, and when my mother sees him in passing in the driveway, she says he asks about me. I know he's disappointed with the choices I've made and I hope that in time he'll come around. My mother though—she's a completely different person since she kicked my father out.

"Lorelei, I think I finally settled on a tattoo," she tells me, walking up to Dallas and me.

I feel the rumble of Dallas's laughter against my back and I elbow him in the ribs.

She holds out a piece of paper and I take it from her hand. "I like the idea of getting song lyrics like you did, but I couldn't find any I liked. I saw this neat little slogan and I thought it was perfect. I don't know if it's got anything to do with me, but I don't care; I still want it."

Glancing down at the paper in my hands, I laugh so hard that my sides hurt and tears start to roll down my cheeks. Kennedy and Paige walk over to see what's going on. I silently hand them the piece of paper.

"My mom's new tattoo, what do you guys think?" I ask them through my laughter.

"Oh, my God. This is fucking epic! I think we should all get this tattooed on our asses," Kennedy laughs, handing the paper to Paige.

She reads it over quickly and giggles. "Oh, this is perfect. Mrs. Warner, you are a genius. We're definitely going with you."

Dallas holds his hand out for the paper and Paige gives it to him. He reads it out loud. "Fool me once, shame on you. Fool me twice . . . I don't fucking think so."

This just makes us all dissolve into laughter again.

"I think this should be our slogan. I'm going to get a new sign made for the front of the building," Kennedy says.

"We were fools once, but never again," Paige announces.

"Shame on you two for thinking that opening this business would never work," Kennedy tells us with a shake of her head.

Paige nods in agreement. "Shame on me for not believing we could do this."

They both look at me and smile. "And shame on all the fucking 'hims' in our lives for screwing us over!"

The three of us cheer and clink our glasses together.

We were all fooled at one point in our lives, but I guess we should be thankful for that. Without those idiot men in our lives, we'd never be where we are today—with a successful business and blissfully in love all over again.

ACKNOWLEDGMENTS

To the team at Amazon, especially JoVon and Krista, thank you for all of your support and hard work to make this series everything I imagined it to be. I enjoyed every moment of working with you!

To Donna, my rock and my reason for not going completely insane on a daily basis, thank you for always answering my crazy texts at all hours of the day and for talking me down from the ledge on more than one occasion.

To Tina, thank you for Long Island Ice Tea nights and for letting me be "just Tara" with you. I will forever be grateful for your support and girl time. I love you!

To Tara's Tramps, for being the best group of crazies I've ever known! Thank you for your unwavering support and inappropriateness that makes me feel less insane than I really am.

For all the blogs, fellow authors, and fans who share my work with others—you are the reason I've been able to follow my dream. Thank you from the bottom of my heart for your love and support.

ABOUT THE AUTHOR

Tara Sivec is a *USA Today* best-selling author, wife, mother, chauffeur, maid, short-order cook, babysitter, and sarcasm expert. She lives in Ohio with her husband and two children and looks forward to the day when all three of them become adults and move out.

After working in the brokerage business for fourteen years, Tara decided to pick up a pen and write instead of shoving it in her eye out of boredom. She is the author of the Playing with Fire series and the Chocolate Lovers series. Her novel *Seduction and Snacks* won first place in the Indie Romance Convention Readers Choice Awards 2013 for Best Indie First Book.

In her spare time, Tara loves to dream about all of the baking she'll do and naps she'll take when she ever gets spare time.

For information on Tara Sivec's work, visit www.tarasivec.com.